Broad Reach 4/7/15

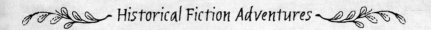

The Devil's Door

A Salem Witchcraft Story

Paul B. Thompson

Enslow Publishers, Inc.
40 Industrial Road
Box 398
Berkeley Heights, NJ 07922
USA
http://www.enslow.com

For Lucy

Library of Congress Cataloging-in-Publication Data:

Thompson, Paul B.
    The devil's door : a Salem witchcraft story / Paul B. Thompson.
        p. cm. — (Historical fiction adventures (HFA))
    Summary: Sarah Wright and her father Ephraim move to Salem Village, Massachusetts, in 1692, where they witness the Salem witchcraft hysteria, during which Ephraim is arrested and Sarah must try to help him escape from jail.
    Includes bibliographical references (p.   )
    ISBN 978-0-7660-3387-0 (Library Ed.)
    ISBN 978-1-59845-214-3 (Paperback Ed.)
    1. Trials (Witchcraft)—Massachusetts—Salem—Juvenile fiction. [1. Trials (Witchcraft)—Fiction. 2. Witchcraft—Fiction. 3. Puritans—Fiction. 4. Fathers and daughters—Fiction. 5. Salem (Mass.)—History—Colonial period, ca. 1600-1775—Fiction.] I. Title.
    PZ7.T3719828De 2010
    [Fic]—dc22
                        2009040374

Printed in the United States of America

062010 Lake Book Manufacturing, Inc., Melrose Park, IL

10 9 8 7 6 5 4 3 2 1

Illustration Credits: © Jupiterimages Corporation, p. 156; Library of Congress, pp. 157, 158; © North Wind Picture Archives, p. 159; Original Painting by © Corey Wolfe, p. 1.

Cover Illustration: Original Painting by © Corey Wolfe.

Contents

chapter one

The Sunlit Path

If Mankind have thus far once consented unto the credit
of Diabolical representations, the Door is opened!

—Cotton Mather

Sarah had the dream again, despite her many prayers. It was always the same. She awoke in her family's house in the Eastward. The house was eerily quiet and empty. Sunlight shone through the open door.

She threw back the quilt. Motes of dust whirled in the shaft of sunlight dividing the one-room house. No fire blazed in the fireplace. There was no sign of her father, Ephraim, her mother, Mary, or her brother, Simon. For some reason she did not call out to them. Throughout the dream she never spoke a word.

Wearing only her shift, she went to the open door. Outside, the yard was completely empty. Where was the dusty brown rooster who could not crow on key? Where was Simon's dog, Kip? She stepped over the log threshold into bright daylight.

The morning was hot, strange weather for so late in the year. Joseph Strong, who farmed the land over the hill, called it "Indian summer." Sarah had heard the Wabanaki Indians practiced sorcery. Their powwows, or wizards, made pacts with the Devil to gain power over the weather.

She looked in the barn, which was just a shed tacked onto the end of the house. It was as quiet as a tomb. The pigs usually squealed loudly when anyone approached. She saw why the barn was so still: All the animals were gone. The only thing Sarah found was a single brown egg nestled in the straw. It was still warm.

Her heart raced with sudden fear. Where was everyone? Her father should be in the cornfield at this hour. He would know where everyone was.

Sarah walked, barefoot in her linen shift, down to the big maple tree. Its leaves were already gilded yellow. At the maple, the path forked. Straight ahead the path led down the hill, through the fallow field to the woods. Beyond the woods lay the Casco River. To the right were her family's fields. Sarah went that way.

Grasshoppers stirred as she kicked through the weeds. They fluttered away, brown as dead leaves. Flying slowly in dream-silence, they were the only living things she saw.

Shriveled and brown, the corn stood a foot higher than Sarah's head. Her father and brother had been cutting dead stalks and binding them into sheaves, but the work was only half done. There was no sign of Ephraim or Simon.

Something on the ground glinted in the strong sunlight. Sarah found her father's sickle lying in the dirt. Her father would never leave a valuable tool on the ground. She picked it up.

An unrecognizable sound brought her around. It might have been a birdcall, a shout, or a scream. The dream-silence was so profound Sarah did not know what she heard, if anything. She wandered back through the soldierly rows of dried corn to the path. There was a ditch at the far end, lined with a blackberry hedge, and on the other side of that the garden patch where the Wrights grew squash and beans. Still holding the sickle, Sarah started toward the ditch.

Halfway there, she faltered. Staring at the sunlit gap in the blackberry hedge, Sarah knew she could not go any farther. There was something on the other side of the ditch, something terrible. The gap in the hedge beckoned like an open door. She could see nothing, but she knew it was there. Death was beyond the blackberries. Death, and the Devil awaited her.

The smothering silence ended like a clap of thunder. The sickle fell from Sarah's hand. There were stains on the blade she had not seen before.

Run! Run! Run, to save your life!

Hitching up her shift, Sarah ran. Her first thought was to get to the house, but by the time she reached the maple tree, a strong smell of smoke filled the air. Smoke was rising from the house— more smoke than ever came from the chimney. Sarah turned and ran to the unplanted field. She had long legs and could run like a deer. The wind tore her cap from her head, releasing a stream of honey-colored hair. She wanted to look back, but did not dare.

She quickly reached the woods. Goodman Strong's cows foraged there, trampling the underbrush until it was easy to run through. She heard the snap of twigs breaking behind her. Every sound was a stab in the back. Sarah plunged on, ducking under the low branches in her way.

Abruptly, she burst out of the trees, at the top of a steep hill. She almost fell. Waving her arms, she threw herself against a nearby boulder. Sarah clung to the sun-warmed stone, feeling every beat of her heart against her ribs. Her father and Joseph Strong had laid stone on the slope to make steps. At the bottom of the hill was a narrow, muddy beach. Every few weeks a boat came up from Casco Bay, bringing messages from the Bay Colony and goods for sale or trade.

Whatever was behind her was still coming. Twigs cracked and branches snapped all around her. Sarah pushed off the rock.

Halfway down the hill Sarah heard shouts from below. The boat was there. It was a big craft with high, pointed ends, manned by six rowers and a steersman. Sarah could see many people crowded into it. One was standing and waving furiously at her.

The sharp rock slabs cut her feet. Smears of red stained every step. Voices from the boat were calling, "Come on, come on, don't stop." At one point she slipped, sprawling on her face. Then she heard someone call, "Sarah, Sarah, get up!" It was her father.

She scrambled up, and in two hops reached the little beach at the foot of the hill. Cold mud felt like balm on her torn feet. Leaning her hands on her knees to gasp for breath, Sarah was amazed to see a man in a steel helmet stand up in the boat. He raised a long musket, sighted along the barrel, and fired.

Flint scraped steel. She saw the priming flash, but did not hear the shot. Everyone in the boat was shouting now, calling her, begging her to come. Sarah waded into the cold stream. She knew how to swim, but no one could swim far with a wet shift on. Sarah waded and waded until the water was up to her chin. The people in the boat begged her to hurry.

A second man in the boat rose, shouldered a musket, and fired. This time the blast rocked her. She slipped and went under.

She was hauled, spitting, to the surface. Her father had her. Ephraim Wright heaved his daughter into the boat. Sarah landed in the laps of people she did not know. The women's faces were streaked with soot. Tears cut tracks in the black dust. Already the oars were biting the water. The boat pulled away from shore.

The last part of Sarah's dream was always the same. She sat up, gripping the side of the boat to steady herself. She looked back at the landing. Standing there were three men. A fourth lay sprawled on the steps, unmoving. They were Wabanaki warriors. Two clad in long buckskin shirts waved war clubs over their heads and howled like demons. It was the silent one, however, who haunted Sarah's sleep from that moment on. He was a great, muscular man, bare to the waist, with his head shaved except for a narrow scalp lock. Half of his face and chest was painted blood red, and the other half was dead black. In his hand was a long knife. He stared at the retreating boat, directly into Sarah's eyes.

No, it was not a knife the fearsome warrior held. It was her father's sickle, stained red like his chest.

Sarah awoke with a start. The room was cold and dark, a long way from her home in the Eastward, that part of the Massachusetts Bay Colony also called Maine. It was February 1692. There was nothing to fear. Maine was far away. She was on board the good ship *William,* bound for Massachusetts Bay.

chapter two

Winter Winds

The sea was as gray as the sky the morning the brig *William* dropped its anchor in Gloucester harbor. It had been a dreary passage from Maine, under pelting rain and sleet all the way.

William carried forty-four settlers who had lost their homes to raiding Indians. Like Ephraim Wright, they had farms along the Saco or Casco rivers. Wabanaki attacks had driven the colonists to fortified coastal towns. The Wrights ended up in Wells. After unbearable weeks of charity, most of the settlers decided to leave.

The minister at Wells, Reverend Burroughs, asked Ephraim to stay. Before coming to America, Sarah's father had been a soldier. He had fought the French and the Spanish in the Old World. After many campaigns, Ephraim left England with his family to find peace in the New World.

"You are a fighting man," Reverend Burroughs said. "Stay and help us fight the devilish Indians." He boasted he could get Ephraim a commission in the Wells Militia.

"I cannot stay, reverend sir," Ephraim said. "My daughter needs a safe home."

Reverend Burroughs patted Sarah on the cheek. She shrank from his touch. A short man with broad shoulders, Burroughs wore hats with brims too wide and crowns too tall. He stood too close to people, talked loudly, and spoke to her father as if he were a servant. For a man of God, he was lordly and overbearing, not a humble minister of the gospel.

"Lamb, where are your manners?" Ephraim asked. Lamb was his pet name for her.

Sarah held on to her father's hand. "Begging your pardon."

Burroughs laughed. He asked, "Where will you go, Goodman Wright?"

"To the Bay Colony."

They had little choice. The Wrights were penniless. The royal government offered free passage to displaced settlers, but only as far as Massachusetts.

So the Wrights were in sad company on the *William*. Sarah was the only child on board. She spent much of the voyage on deck, despite the weather. Below deck was stifling, and many of their fellow passengers groaned or shrieked in their sleep. They were all widows or old men. The Wabanaki killed men and boys of fighting age, and carried off young women and children as hostages. Mothers and fathers who had lost their children gazed at Sarah so forlornly that she stayed on deck, never more than arm's length from her father.

They went ashore in Gloucester. People lined the dock, seeking news of the war. Ephraim and Sarah hurried down the plank and pushed their way through the crowd, avoiding all questions. Once through the press, Ephraim stopped.

Sarah cast about, adrift. "Where do we go?"

Ephraim looked perplexed for a moment, then brightened when he recognized a man across the street.

He hailed him. "Roger! Roger Fanthorpe! *Corporal!*"

A burly, mustached man wearing a sword on his hip turned around.

"Private Wright! Is that you?"

"Come on, lamb," her father said, steering Sarah ahead of him. They crossed the narrow, muddy street to where the man waited.

The men clasped hands. "How are you, corporal?" Ephraim asked.

"Corporal no longer, if you please! You see before you Sergeant Fanthorpe of the Gloucester Militia. Merciful God, Wright, I haven't seen you since Sedgemoor! Rum fight, that one. Remember how you shot that Dutchman off his horse—?"

Ephraim cleared his throat. Sarah looked from Fanthorpe, with his red face and curling mustache, to her pale, exhausted father. Ephraim seldom talked about his soldiering days. War was a sinful business, he said. The past was something Ephraim was striving mightily to amend.

Fanthorpe gave Sarah a glance. "Ancient history, what? What brought you to the colonies?"

"Land. Peace." The words were bitter on his lips. "I had a holding in the Eastward, lost now to the Wabanaki."

His few words spoke volumes to the worldly sergeant. He clapped Ephraim on the shoulder.

"My dear friend," he said. "Are you at loose ends?"

Ephraim put his arm around Sarah. "All we are, and all we have, you see before you."

"Into the Ordinary then, and break your fast! Come!" Fanthorpe herded father and daughter into the nearby door of Wilkins' Ordinary, an inn off the waterfront. It was warm inside, with a good blaze in the fireplace.

Fanthorpe shouted for service. "Beer! Bread! And hot soup! Jump to it!"

The innkeeper bellowed back in agreement. Fanthorpe steered the Wrights to a table and sat them down. Food arrived quickly. Sarah said a brief, silent prayer and dug in. The thick corn soup warmed her down to her toes.

"So, Ephraim," Fanthorpe said, leaning back, hands clasped across his barrel chest. "What will you do now?"

"I know not."

"Come back to soldiering! I can find a place in my company for you."

Ephraim shook his head. "I am no longer a soldier. I am a farmer."

"New England is full of farmers starving to death, but a good soldier can always find employment, especially in dark times."

"I am no longer a soldier," Ephraim repeated. "I heard the word of God to sow and reap, not kill my fellow men." Sarah noticed he used the same tone with his old comrade that he used on her when he would have no more argument.

Fanthorpe shrugged. "If you are determined to toil like any witless oaf, I can at least point you to a place where there is land to work. Do you know Salem Town?"

Everyone in New England knew Salem. It was a goodly town, second only to Boston in size and wealth.

"North of the town there's some tracts called Salem Farms. A number of souls driven from the Eastward have gone there seeking a livelihood."

"Good land, is it?"

Fanthorpe gulped his beer. "Have not seen it myself. Probably all stones, weeds, and Non-Conformists."

Fanthorpe belonged to the Church of England. Massachusetts was still a stronghold of the Non-Conformists, or Puritans, as they were often called. Not so long ago, if settlers did not profess the gospel of the Non-Conformists, they could not vote or own land in the Bay Colony. Since the Restoration of King Charles II in 1660, the hold of the Puritans had loosened a good deal.

"Any other places worth considering?" asked Ephraim.

"There's a number of townships in those parts crying for the plow," Fanthorpe replied. "Andover, Topsfield, Rowley. Take your pick."

A street crier passed Wilkins' Ordinary, calling the hour. Fanthorpe muttered an oath. He got up, excusing himself.

"Our company musters this morning," he explained. "Word is we shall be called to service in the Eastward at any time."

"God go with you," Ephraim said. He offered his hand. Fanthorpe dug into his belt and slipped his old comrade some coins. Sarah's father protested.

"Nonsense! When you become a wealthy gentleman farmer, you may pay me back twice the amount, eh?"

"My daughter and I thank you."

The sergeant clucked his tongue. "Nothing to it, old fellow. Farewell, child." He chucked Sarah under the chin. She managed a thin smile.

The crier repeated his call. "God's blood, I must fly. If things don't work out farming, seek me out, Wright. I will save you a place in the Gloucester Company!"

When Fanthorpe was gone, Ephraim said to Sarah, "He's a good fellow."

Sarah was not so sure. For a moment she feared her father would accept Fanthorpe's offer to join the militia.

"Time to go," he said, draining his mug.

"Go where, Father?"

"Salem Farms. It is too early to plant, but someone may take me on as a laborer. We must eat, and I will take no more charity!"

With the smell of the sea still on them, the Wrights set out for Salem Farms, or Salem Village, as it was also known. Getting there was their first problem. Fanthorpe's money—a few shillings—they needed for food and lodging. There was not enough to spare to hire a horse.

It took a half day's search on the waterfront for Ephraim to find a freight wagon bound for Salem Town. The teamster agreed to let the Wrights ride along without charge once he heard they were refugees from the Eastward.

Down a muddy, rutted road they rolled. The Wrights had to ride in the back of the wagon against a line of kegs. Ephraim nodded, catching up on the rest he had denied himself since leaving Casco Bay. Sarah huddled under her father's arm. Sleet stung her face as she watched the countryside unfold behind them.

The road to Salem was lined with vacant fields and barren trees, their limbs naked against the sky. Livestock had been driven in to escape the weather, and the cornfields were populated by sheaves of brittle brown stalks, scattered about like the columns of some ancient ruin.

The only living things Sarah saw were crows. As many as a dozen black birds perched in a single tree, watching the girl watching them. They reminded Sarah of the Wabanaki, hidden in the Maine woods, waiting to strike.

Her father stirred. "Here, what's this?" He put a dry, leathery hand to her cheek to stop the tears.

"It's the cold," Sarah said. "How soon will we get there?"

Ephraim asked the wagoneer. "Soon, soon," he said.

Ephraim sang a hymn to pass the time. He was a strong but tuneless baritone. Sarah joined the refrain in her lighter, more pleasing voice. In short order the sleet ceased and the sun broke through the mantle of clouds. Such was the power of praising God, Sarah decided.

They reached a crossroads. The old man hauled back on the reins. "Here's my turn," he said. "You get off here. The Farms are dead ahead."

Ephraim and Sarah thanked him. Without a second glance, the driver cracked his whip and moved on.

"How far is it to the village?" Sarah wondered.

"Not far, I hope." Ephraim buttoned his coat and retied the scarf around his neck. "If we start now, we might be there before sundown."

It was already well past noon. A bitter wind blew from the north. Sarah dropped her chin to her chest. Eyes half-closed, she trailed a few steps behind her father. He gallantly shielded her from the wind. They tramped a long way in silence.

At last Ephraim said, "Look, Sarah. A bridge!"

Ahead a stone bridge spanned a quick-flowing stream. Beyond the bridge were the first dwellings they had seen in miles.

Six houses, widely spaced, lined the right side of the road. They were modest, weathered farmhouses. Fieldstone chimneys sent plumes of smoke into the frigid sky. Fences surrounded each holding, but the yards were empty. Across the road were two large pastures. Set well back in the midst of one was a lone house.

Ephraim went to the door of the first home and knocked. Though smoke rose from the flue, no one answered Ephraim's rapping. Nor did anyone appear at the second house.

His face set hard with frustration. Where was Christian hospitality in this place?

Approaching the third house, Ephraim and Sarah were surprised to hear laughter and loud voices coming from within. Ephraim knocked. At once the door flew open. Warmth and the smell of ale wafted out.

"Enter, friends, ere you perish!"

Ephraim led Sarah inside. The house was bigger than the previous ones, and better finished, though unpainted. The house was a small tavern. A roaring fire filled the broad hearth. Four men were there, seated around a table. They had a game between them. Sarah had never seen it before, but her father knew it well from his soldiering days. It was called shovel-board. Coins were pushed back and forth across the board. Whoever got their coin closest to a certain line painted on the board—but not over it—won the wager.

The men looked like farmers, with dirty boots and homespun shirts. The woman who had opened the door was altogether different. She was tall, and she had black hair streaked with silver. Her clothes were grander than anything Sarah had ever seen: a black skirt and a red bodice, with great swatches of white lace on the cuffs and hem. She wore a cap, but it was not the starched white headpiece Sarah was used to. Their hostess wore a small black cap, pinned well forward and set at a jaunty angle.

"Poor wretches!" she said. "Half chilled to death!" She laid a hand on Ephraim's arm in a familiar manner.

"We'll fix you up. Boston ale for you, goodman?" She cupped Sarah's cheek in her hand. "Your skin is like ice! Hot cider for the girl, eh?"

Ephraim and Sarah sat down by the fire. While the heat burrowed through their clothes, the grandly dressed woman returned, bearing two steaming cups.

"Hold, goodwife. I have little money," Ephraim said. Sarah bit her lip. She could smell the cider. It was piping hot and laced with spices.

Their hostess smiled. She had uncommonly fine white teeth.

"Perhaps you would like to try your hand at our game? You might win enough for supper for you and the child," she said.

Ephraim politely declined. "I have seen too many men lose the shirt off their back playing shovel-board."

"Have you, now? You must be a man of the world. You don't talk like a sailor, so I'll wager you were a soldier."

"I was, goodwife, in a former time."

She set the hot mugs down beside Ephraim and Sarah. "I am Bridget Bishop. Welcome to Salem Village."

Ephraim gave his name and Sarah's. "We've come from the Eastward."

That silenced the men at the table. "In sooth, you are from there? How goes the war?" asked a young man.

"There's fighting enough, but it is not war." Ephraim picked up the mug and took a sip. Sarah tugged at his cuff until he agreed she could have the cider. Between sips he described conditions in Maine. Wabanaki war parties slipped out of the woods to steal cattle and sack farms. After they struck, the colonial militia floundered after them, seldom catching a glimpse of the raiders.

His account filled the house with silence. Goodwife Bishop broke it with a loud laugh.

"You are out of it now, Goodman Wright!" She tried to talk Ephraim into ordering food, but he refused.

"I was told there might be work around here," he said. "Is anyone in the village looking for help?"

No one spoke up until Goody Bishop said, "Dr. Griggs is adding to his house. I'll wager he could use a good carpenter."

"Where can I find Dr. Griggs?"

"Half a mile down the road, below Leach's Hill."

Ephraim drained his cup and urged Sarah to finish. When their hostess quoted her price, Ephraim blanched. He paid it without complaint, even though it was several times the going rate.

He and Sarah went to the door. On his way out he asked to see the shovel-board. Goody Bishop objected, but the oldest farmer dumped the coins off and handed it to Ephraim.

He held it up obliquely, squinting at the board against the firelight.

"There's wax on one end of the board," he said calmly. He handed the game back to the elder man, who evidently had lost a sum to the others. The old farmer scratched the wood with his thumbnail.

"Wax!" he cried. Wax on one end of the board meant coins sliding that way would go farther than they did on the other end.

Stools clattered over as the players leaped to their feet. Ephraim shooed Sarah outside. Bridget Bishop started shouting, but Ephraim slammed the door shut.

"What was that?" Sarah said, hearing a loud crash inside.

"The wages of sin," Ephraim answered, though he smiled when he said it.

chapter three

Whispers and Shadows

Outside, snow lay like shadows on the shaded sides of walls and fence posts. The sun managed to peek through the patchwork of gray clouds cloaking the sky. Sarah remembered the warmth of Goody Bishop's fire and hoped Dr. Griggs had his own blazing.

The knoll ahead had to be Leach's Hill. Rounding it, the Wrights spied a good-sized house, screened by a closely growing orchard. It was being enlarged. The new end of the house was still bare posts and naked rafters. The chimney at the other end was smoking.

There was a sign halfway between the front door and the road. Sarah could read the name W. GRIGGS well enough, but there was a hard word below the name. She asked her father what it said.

"Doctor of Physick," Ephraim replied. "This is the man we seek."

He knocked firmly. They heard voices, muffled by the walls of the house. At last the door opened, held by a plump teenage girl with auburn hair and many freckles.

"Good day," Ephraim said. "Is Dr. Griggs within?"

"You sick?" said the girl.

"Who is it, Betty?" shouted a man from within the house.

"Someone asking for you!" she yelled back.

"Patients?"

"You sick?" the girl repeated.

"No," said Ephraim. "I am newly come to the village. I am looking for work. I was told I might find some here."

The door was snatched open. An elderly man of no great height with deep pockmarks on his cheeks stood there in his waistcoat. He wore a gentleman's wig gone gray from lack of powder.

"They're not sick," said Betty.

"Back to the kitchen with you," the man answered. The apple-cheeked girl vanished inside.

Dr. Griggs eyed Ephraim and Sarah. "I have no time for beggars," he said coldly.

Gripping his daughter's hand, Ephraim stood up ramrod straight. "We are not beggars, sir. I seek work and lodging. If you have neither, we'll not trouble you."

Ephraim turned away.

"Hold," said the doctor. "You have the way of an honest man. Who are you?"

Her father flashed a wink at Sarah. "Ephraim Wright, formerly of Casco Bay, and late of His Majesty's army. This is my daughter, Sarah."

Cold to her toes again, Sarah managed to curtsy. Dr. Griggs smiled, pleased by their manners.

"Soldier, eh? Lately come from the Eastward? Come in, my boy, come in."

Ephraim ducked through the door into a low-ceilinged room. Sarah felt warmth on her face and followed with relief.

A plump, pleasant-looking woman appeared, holding needlework. Dr. Griggs introduced her as his wife, Rachel. The girl who answered the door was their servant, Mrs. Griggs' grandniece, Betty Hubbard.

Goodwife Griggs led them to the fireplace. Sarah sat on the hearth with her back to the flames. Her father and the doctor remained standing.

"Bad business in the Eastward, we hear," Dr. Griggs began.

"I lost my holding, so I thought to lease land in Essex County and begin again," Ephraim said. "As it is too early to plant, I need to work for my keep till spring."

Dr. Griggs warily agreed. He went on at length about how hard it was to get good help in Salem Village. There was a labor shortage all right. Everyone with wits or ambition went to Salem Town to work. What could Ephraim do?

He listed his skills: carpentry, shingle making, raising animals, and a little light blacksmithing.

Sarah was surprised. Her father could do most things he turned his hand to, but she had never seen him forge iron or tend any animals larger than a pig.

While listening to the men, Sarah became aware she was being watched. She looked around. The Griggses had a loft overlooking the main room. Betty gazed down at her between the loft rails. She stared at Sarah with unconcealed hostility. Annoyed, Sarah glared back. Betty's lip stuck out so far a fly could have landed on it. The idea made Sarah smile. Bested by the new girl's grin, Betty's round face vanished.

"I can offer little pay," Dr. Griggs was saying, "but the keep of you and your daughter."

Ephraim accepted. He called Sarah. "We have a roof over us again," he said. "Thank the doctor, Sarah."

"Thank you, sir."

Sarah and her father were to sleep in the loft. While the doctor showed Ephraim what type of work needed to be done on the extension, Sarah climbed the steep steps—a ladder, really—to the loft. There was nothing up there but a long pallet, covered with a straw-stuffed mattress. Light from the hearth cast odd shadows on the ceiling. Sarah worked her way down, wondering where she would sleep.

Betty popped out of the mound of blankets. She looked pleased when Sarah cried out in alarm.

"Nervous, aren't you?" she said.

"You startled me."

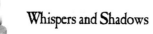

"You are lucky it was only me." Betty lowered her voice to a whisper. "There are bad things abroad 'round here. Evil things."

Sarah knelt on the pallet. "What do you mean?"

"Spirits and devils walk among us . . . "

Goody Griggs called from below. Betty slid past Sarah, frowning deeply. "You will see."

Goody Griggs dispatched Betty on an errand. With her father busy and the peculiar Betty Hubbard gone, Sarah lay down and slept. Walking for miles in the cold had worn her out, and it was good to have a warm spot to lay her head.

When she awoke later, it was night. The dark New England winter filled the house like smoke.

Below, the household was assembled for supper. Dr. and Goody Griggs sat at one end of the family table. At the opposite end sat her father. He had his coat off and his sleeves rolled up. It was the first time in many days Sarah had seen him so relaxed.

Betty Hubbard stirred a pot before the fire. She served her master and mistress first, then Ephraim, ladling soup into shallow wooden bowls.

Ephraim glanced up and saw Sarah. "Come down, lamb," he called. "Supper is ready."

She descended the steep ladder. Her father gestured to the empty bench on his left, facing the fire. Sarah sat down. Before she could speak, Betty dropped a bowl in front of her. It landed with a loud clunk, but it did not spill because it held so little soup.

"Betty! Mind your manners!" Goody Griggs said.

"Yes'm." Sulking, she returned to the hearth to eat her dinner. Sarah realized she had been given Betty's place at the table.

"Once the roof is closed in, the rest of the work will be easy," Ephraim remarked.

"Excellent!" the doctor said.

While the men talked, Sarah and Goody Griggs ate in silence. Now and then the doctor signaled Betty to refill bowls or cups as needed.

"You are heaven-sent, Goodman Wright," Dr. Griggs announced. "With your help I shall have the finest house in the village."

"What about the Putnams?" asked Betty.

"Hush, child!" Goody Griggs said. "No one wants to hear your opinion."

"Sergeant Putnam's house is very nice," Betty said stubbornly. Goody Griggs waved Betty over, then slapped her. Downcast, Betty mumbled an apology and returned to the hearth.

"It is hard having a kinswoman as a servant," Dr. Griggs said. "We bought her indenture out of kindness, but Betty gives herself such airs."

For the first time Sarah felt sorry for Betty Hubbard. Her mother had not struck her in years, and as far as she could remember, her father never had.

Ephraim asked about the spiritual life of the village. Where was the meetinghouse? Who was the minister?

The meetinghouse was about two miles away, in the heart of the village, Dr. Griggs said. "As for the minister, his name is Samuel Parris. He came to us from the West Indies three years ago."

"Is he a good preacher?"

The doctor looked thoughtful. "He is devoted to our Lord in every way."

That did not answer his question, but Ephraim let the matter rest. They would go to meeting in two days and see for themselves.

Everyone went to bed after supper—everyone but Betty, whose job was to clean up. Sarah mounted the steps to the loft. She undressed down to her shift, crawled onto the pallet, and drew the covers up to her chin.

Sleep was hard to find. Strange shadows played upon the ceiling, and Betty Hubbard was not careful with the pots and plates. They clattered loudly until Dr. Griggs bellowed from his bed for quiet.

Quiet it became, and everyone fell asleep—everyone but Sarah. Maybe it was her nap earlier, but she found it hard to rest. Would she have that dream again? She prayed earnestly for blank, empty sleep.

Her eyes had almost closed when she heard a strange sound from below. Snapping awake, Sarah heard Betty muttering in a curious, singsong manner. Then she heard whispers along with the chanting. Someone else was with Betty.

Sarah crawled under the cover to the end of the bed. Her father snored lightly a few feet away, oblivious. Lifting the blanket, Sarah peeked through the loft rail.

Two figures huddled before the fire. The shorter, thicker one she guessed was Betty. Beside her was a taller, slimmer girl about the same age.

"Now throw it in the fire," whispered the other girl. Betty's hand darted out, tossing something into the flames. There was a pop, and the girls recoiled.

Dr. Griggs mumbled loudly from the darkened end of the room. Taking fright, the girls hurried to the door. The stranger went out, leaving Betty to shut the door. Sarah crept back to her place.

A moment later, Betty eased past the Wrights. She stopped at Sarah's feet.

"Mind your own business, girl," she muttered, "or someone will put out those spying eyes!"

Sarah swallowed hard. How did Betty know she was awake? She felt the older girl slip into bed at the far end of the pallet. The fire below died away, leaving the house in darkness.

chapter four

Meetinghouse

The sun was shining the morning they walked to meeting. It was cold, but the glare melted the ice on fence rails and tree limbs, causing a steady sprinkle of cold, bright drops. Sarah had to hurry to keep up with her father.

Ahead of them walked Dr. Griggs and his wife in their best clothes. Dr. Griggs used a long-handled cane, like a fashionable doctor in London might carry, but the knob on his cane was brass, not gold. Goody Griggs wore a pretty blue shawl across her shoulders.

Behind the Wrights came Betty Hubbard. She had her arms crossed high on her chest, and her chin thrust down to her wrists. Goody Griggs had chastised her twice that morning, once for laziness and again for scorching the porridge.

They met more people on the road. Dr. Griggs tipped his tall hat to the men he met. Everyone looked over the Wrights, but no one said more than "Good morning, goodman" to them.

They left the main road for a narrower, well-worn path. A number of families fell in with them. Sarah studied them, being careful not to stare. The men were sturdy farmers, with faces and hands made hard by wind and sun. She saw a few old widows, thin and paper-skinned, clinging to a grown son's strong arm.

Sarah was most interested in the children. There were more children in Salem Village than Sarah had ever seen. She saw babies in arms, toddlers clinging to an elder's hand, and older children walking dutifully behind their parents. Girls seemed to outnumber boys. She saw very few young men. Sarah realized many of them must have already gone to serve with the militia in Maine.

Three girls fell in behind Sarah, talking in hushed tones with Betty Hubbard. The tall one Sarah thought might have been the one who was in the Griggs house last night, but she could not be sure. When Betty spotted Sarah looking at them, she stuck out her tongue. Unfortunately, Goody Griggs happened to be looking her way just then.

"Foolish girl, what if the Lord froze your face in such a devilish grimace? What would you do then?"

Be a gargoyle on a church roof, Sarah thought, but did not say.

As they neared the meetinghouse, a swarm of boys ran past, shouting and kicking up mud from their heels. Some got on Sarah's dress.

"Hello!" she said, vexed. "What are you doing?"

Three of the boys kept running, but the trailing one stopped. He was no stranger to mud. Spots of brown and red earth speckled his pants and coat.

"Sorry," said the boy. He had sky blue eyes, an upturned nose, and a wild thatch of black hair barely contained by a battered felt cap.

He waited for Sarah to catch up. "Haven't seen you before," he said.

Sarah walked past him without reply. The boy grinned.

"Sorry about the mud," he said again.

"Be more careful," Sarah said primly.

"I will."

She walked faster. Her father had gone ahead by a half-dozen steps, and she did not want to be too far from him.

"My name's Absalom Toothaker," he said, skipping to keep up with her. "Most folks call me Abe."

"It is easier to say."

"What's your name?"

"Sarah Wright."

"Pleased to meet you, Sarah Wright."

Ephraim had reached the meetinghouse. He called for Sarah to join him. She hurried quickly to him, and they entered together. Sarah looked back, but Abe was no longer in sight.

It was a fair-sized place, with a wooden pulpit and a few benches up front, where the leaders of the community and their families sat. Most people were expected to stand. Being newcomers, Ephraim and Sarah went to the back. An assortment of people joined them at the rear of the room: young mothers with noisy babies, folks in torn and patched clothing, and a few ancients leaning on canes.

At the pulpit stood the minister, Reverend Parris. A little older than Ephraim Wright, his preacher's robe had faded from black to dark gray. Holes in the elbows were neatly darned. Reverend Parris surveyed the congregation with a slight frown, tapping a finger against the cover of his prayer book. He had restless eyes, and constantly flexed his lips. To Sarah he looked more like a merchant than a man of God.

"May the good Lord bless you and keep you!" he intoned. He opened his Bible and read from Psalm 110: "'The Lord said unto my Lord, Sit thou at my right hand, until I make thine enemies thy footstool. The Lord shall send the rod of thy strength out of Zion; rule thou in the midst of thine enemies.'"

He went on, reaching a verse that struck Sarah hard, considering recent events: "'He shall judge among the heathen, he shall fill the places with the dead bodies; he shall wound the heads over many countries.'"

People on the front bench began to stir and mutter. Parris ignored them. Then a girl sitting down front let out a most unchurchly yelp. The woman beside her—her mother, surely— tried to calm her, but the girl let out another resounding whoop.

After the second cry, another girl near the front gave a loud groan. She threw up her hands, stood, and shouted, "Yah! Yah! Yah!" again and again, even when an anguished-looking man tried to pull her back to the bench.

What was going on here?

Betty Hubbard, being a servant, stood by the side wall. Sarah glanced her way and saw she had her eyes screwed tightly shut. Betty's face was growing redder and redder. The tall girl, her night visitor, was by her side, wan and round-eyed.

Reverend Parris tried to speak over the ruckus, but failed.

"For goodness' sake, take her out," he said. The woman with the first girl dragged her to her feet. She was younger than Sarah, eight or nine, rather pretty in a fragile way. The sounds coming from her lips were not pretty. She screeched and howled while waving clawed fingers at some threat only she could see.

"Keep away! Keep away! I won't sign your book! It's the Devil's book! I won't, I won't, I won't-won't-won't—"

"Take her *out!*" the minister said sternly. Another woman helped drag the screeching child away. Sarah heard people around her murmur, "Poor Betty Parris!"

Removing the first girl did not help the second. She was seated at the front, a well-dressed child about Sarah's age. Leaping up on the bench, the girl flailed her fists in the air. She roared insults when two grave-faced men tried to take hold of her.

"Dirty liar!" she screamed. "Dirty beggar! Don't! Don't!" She lapsed into animal growls again.

Reverend Parris demanded the men take the distracted girl away. At that the second girl screamed piercingly. She held her shriek unwaveringly until a well-dressed man clamped his hand over her mouth.

A fresh disturbance by the wall caught everyone's attention. Peeking through the forest of adults, Sarah saw Betty Hubbard on the floor. Apparently, she had fainted. Everyone was standing now, the meeting totally upset by the bizarre behavior of the girls.

Ephraim caught Sarah's hand. Tugging her along, he made for the door. Most of the congregation was also leaving. Betty Hubbard's tall friend knelt over her, hands clasped in prayer. The shrieking girl was being hustled out of the meetinghouse even as she shouted frightful things at her tormentors.

Outside, in the open air, Sarah drew a deep breath. Ephraim shook his head in wonder. He looked around for Dr. and Goody Griggs.

"I saw them go with Reverend Parris," Sarah said. Manners did not permit the Wrights to return to the Griggs house before their hosts, so they had to wait for the doctor.

Ephraim and Sarah circled the meetinghouse. The first two girls were gone. As the Wrights completed their circuit, they saw Betty Hubbard being carried out by two young men. Dr. and Goody Griggs were waiting for her.

"Stop this nonsense, girl," said Goody Griggs. "You shame us and yourself by such conduct in the Lord's meeting!"

Betty lolled between the two youths, limp as a rag. The doctor cupped her chin in his hand. He turned her head this way and that, peeled back an eyelid, and felt for Betty's pulse.

"This is no ordinary swoon," he declared. Betty was unconscious, but her pulse was racing. Dr. Griggs pinched her earlobe to rouse her. Betty hung completely lifeless between the two men.

Reverend Parris hurried up, his old robe fluttering.

"Doctor! Doctor, you must come to my house at once! My daughter has taken a turn for the worse!"

"How is Abigail?" asked Dr. Griggs, still studying Betty Hubbard closely.

"I don't know," Reverend Parris said tersely. "Will you attend my child?"

Dr. Griggs saw Ephraim Wright standing close by. "I shall wait upon your Betty and send mine home. Goodman Wright!"

Ephraim stepped forward.

"See Mrs. Griggs and this girl home, will you?" Ephraim vowed that he would. "Thank you, Goodman. I shall return as soon as I can."

Ephraim took Betty Hubbard from the youths. He cradled her under her knees and shoulders. Goody Griggs stalked past, barely giving her grandniece a second glance.

Grimacing under his burden, Ephraim said to Sarah, "Follow Goody Griggs."

They tramped home. At the crossroads leading back to Ipswich Road, Sarah saw Abe Toothaker spying on them from a hayrick. Realizing he was seen, the boy beckoned Sarah.

She angled to the edge of the road.

"What do you want?"

"What happened in the meeting?" the boy asked. Sarah described the chaos.

Abe's sharp features darkened. "They're bewitched!"

Her father was now a score of yards ahead. "Bewitched?" she replied. "They could be moonstruck, for all you know."

"My uncle Roger is a doctor. He knows all about sickness and such, and he says those girls are under an evil hand!"

"Sarah . . . " her father called.

She started toward him. "I have to go."

"You'll see," Abe said. "There's witches in these parts. They're partial to girls, and they'll get you if you're not careful!"

Sarah sniffed. Trying to scare her with talk of witches! She had no doubt the Devil had servants in this world, but she was far more afraid of Indian powwows or papists. Who would want to bewitch the minister's daughter or a sullen servant like Betty Hubbard?

Still, there were Betty's late-night deeds to explain. Chanting in the dark, throwing things in the fire smacked of magic, and there was only one kind of magic in the world—the Devil's.

The wind was really gusting by the time they reached home. Betty Hubbard had not stirred the whole time. Goody Griggs asked Ephraim to put the girl on the floor before the fireplace. Then she sternly ordered Betty to rise.

"Get up, you lazy jade! Have you no shame? Rise up, I say!"

Betty did not stir. Mouth pursed in annoyance, Goody Griggs fetched a dipper of water and dashed it on Betty. When the girl still did not respond, she went for another. Ephraim plucked the dipper from her hand.

"Do you mind, goodwife? I am thirsty from my long walk."

Ephraim offered the first sip to Sarah. Up close, she whispered, "Father, what is this?"

"I don't know, lamb." He closed his eyes and drank. "Stay calm and trust in God."

Goody Griggs sat down at the family table and took out her psalm book. Parting the well-thumbed pages, she read aloud, "'Hear my prayer, O Lord, and let my cry come unto thee. Hide not thy face from me in the day when I am in trouble; incline thine ear unto me; in the days when I shall call answer me speedily!'"

She went on, through one psalm to another until Betty sat up. She felt her wet hair and apron.

"Is it raining?" she muttered.

"Only on slothful sinners!" Goody Griggs closed her book and ordered Betty to stoke the fire. Dazed, she obeyed without complaint.

Dr. Griggs was gone for a long time. Snow began to fall at sunset, and the doctor arrived in a two-wheel cart, driven by a swarthy man in a fur coat. The hiss of wheels in the newly fallen snow brought Sarah to the shuttered window. She saw the dark man help Dr. Griggs down from the cart.

"Indian!" she gasped. Ephraim and Goody Griggs came to the window.

"Oh, that's the Parrises' slave, John," she said. "It was good of Reverend Parris to send the doctor home by cart."

She drew back the latch and let her husband in. Dr. Griggs brushed snow from his shoulders and called hoarsely for a hot drink. Betty filled a cup from a kettle simmering by the fire and brought it to her master.

"How is it, William?" said Goody Griggs.

"Worse than ever." The doctor took a long drink of cider. While Betty laid out supper for him, Dr. Griggs shed his damp coat and shoes.

"My art can do nothing for them," he said with a sigh. "Poor child! The evil hand is upon her!"

The house was quiet save for the snapping of the fire. Sarah looked at each adult in turn. Dr. Griggs was exhausted. Goody Griggs' little mouth was set in a hard line. Her father looked sympathetic but puzzled. Then she glanced at Betty. Her eyes were wide with fright. She had bitten her lower lip—bitten it so hard blood was running down her chin.

"Witchcraft?" Betty gasped.

"As certain as death," said Dr. Griggs.

chapter five

Eyes Opened

Ephraim worked hard on the Griggs house. He hauled stone, cut timber, and split shingles when the weather permitted. Sarah stayed by him, fetching tools and passing anything he might need up the ladder where he worked. Though it was often bitterly cold, she could not bear being in the house. Betty Hubbard wandered about, mumbling and sighing. Goody Griggs lectured her, but Betty seemed completely undone by the doctor's diagnosis. Her friends Betty Parris and Abigail Williams—the girl Sarah's age who acted so wildly in meeting— were victims of witchcraft.

Reverend Parris visited several times, usually with a prosperous-looking man Sarah learned was Thomas Putnam. Goodman Putnam was the richest man in the village (according to Goody Griggs), and he had a number of grave conversations with the doctor and Reverend Parris. Ephraim was summoned to meet these important men.

Dr. Griggs did most of the talking. Sarah could not make out what they were saying, but now and then the portly doctor glanced her way, nodding for emphasis.

He laid a hand on Ephraim's shoulder. Her father looked startled, eyebrows raised. Putnam said little, but Reverend Parris joined in, earnestly pleading. In turn the minister and doctor fell silent. All eyes were on Ephraim Wright.

"Sarah, will you come here?"

She picked her way around piles of stone and timber out into the cold sunshine.

"Sarah, would you do a task for Dr. Griggs later today?" Ephraim asked.

"If I can," she replied.

"A man will come from Reverend Parris," the doctor explained. "I want you to go back with him to the minister's house. I have medicine for Betty Parris. I want you to deliver it, along with directions for Goody Parris."

Sarah did not understand. Why not give the message to Reverend Parris, who stood before him? Why not give the medicine to the preacher's servant?

"She will do it," Ephraim said. "Won't you, lamb?" What could Sarah say but yes?

In midafternoon a cart arrived from the parsonage. Sarah was in the cellar, collecting vegetables for Goody Griggs, when they called her. Dr. Griggs met her at the door with a cloth-wrapped bottle and a folded letter.

"Give these to Goody Parris," he said. "Wait for an answer; there's a good girl."

Sarah went out. A two-wheel cart, drawn by a dusty gray mare, waited at the road. As Sarah approached, she saw the driver was the Indian man she'd seen before. He was short, with high, sharp cheekbones, eyes like jet beads, and a flat nose.

The Indian man held out his hand. "Come, missy," he said. "My mistress waits."

Sarah backed up a step and bumped into her father.

"Get on, girl. He will not hurt you."

"John never hurt anyone," he said. He grinned, showing he had no front teeth.

Ephraim boosted Sarah up into the cart. She perched on the end of the bench, as far from John Indian as she could get. John snapped the reins, and the cart lurched away.

"You 'fraid?" said John after a long silence. "Don't be 'fraid of John." He displayed his gap-toothed smile. "John never hurt anybody."

They rolled along. John kept up a running commentary on the land and houses they passed. Sarah said little. Near Crane Creek they passed a woman on the road. Her dress was muddy from the knees down, and she wore a shapeless man's coat. Sarah caught a whiff of tobacco. The woman had the stub of a clay pipe tight in her teeth, and a tiny baby in her arms. That surprised Sarah. From her roadworn appearance, she took the woman to be quite aged.

John Indian drove past the laboring woman without stopping.

Sarah said, "Can't we give the goodwife a ride?"

"Not her," John replied. "She's a bad one."

"But she has a baby!"

He would not be swayed. Sarah looked back again and saw the woman staring at her. Her expression was not pitiable or sad, but hard with anger.

When they reached the minister's house, John got down to help Sarah. She ignored his hand, put her foot on a wheel spoke, and climbed down. With a shrug, John led the horse and cart to a nearby shed.

The Parris house was very modest. No bigger than the original portion of Dr. Griggs' house, like most dwellings in the village it was in need of repair. Even though winter had many weeks to go, the woodpile beside the house was nearly gone.

Sarah knocked. She expected Goodwife Parris, but when the door opened she was startled to see an Indian woman in servant's garb. Under a fresh white turban was a dark face, framed by heavy black eyebrows and a nose like a hawk's bill. She was not much taller than Sarah. In spite of her formidable appearance, she smiled readily and had a warm voice.

"Hello, missy," she said. "What can I do for you?"

"I have medicine and a letter from Dr. Griggs to Goodwife Parris."

The slave woman opened the door wider. "You do? You best come in, then."

Inside the house was chilly and dark. A weak fire flickered at the hearth.

"You must be cold, missy. That man of mine takes his time when he's out!"

She went to the fire and dipped something from a simmering kettle. Handing a steaming cup to Sarah, she added, "I am Tituba."

"Tituba! Tituba!" a voice echoed shrilly. Her smile vanished.

"Be calm, missy, Tituba's coming!" She filled another cup and hurried to the far end of the house, where a child sat up in bed to receive her drink. Sarah recognized Betty Parris from the meetinghouse.

Sarah came closer. "Is Goodwife Parris at home?"

"She's gone to the Putnams'. Don't know when she be back."

Sarah frowned. She was supposed to put the doctor's note in Goody Parris' hand and wait for a reply. How long would she have to wait?

The door flew open, banging loudly against the wall. In swept a girl, her gray cloak flying behind her. Wide-eyed, she charged past Sarah to the foot of Betty Parris' bed.

"Whish!" said the girl, waving her cloak as if it were wings. "Do you see it come in? The yellow bird?"

"Hush, girl. You'll upset Miss Betty!"

The girl whirled, slapping Tituba's face. "Whish!" she cried. "Begone, Devil bird!"

"Abigail," Betty Parris said weakly. "Don't!"

She spun back around and spied Sarah for the first time.

"The yellow bird sees a worm!" she said. Abigail Williams advanced slowly, transfixing the new girl with a pointing finger. An inch from Sarah's nose, Abigail let out a shrill screech. Sarah flinched. Blood rushed to her face and she struck Abigail on the cheek, just as the Williams girl had struck Tituba.

Sarah tensed for a return blow. Instead of attacking, Abigail danced away in slow circles, arms outstretched.

"Whish, whish! Yellow bird flies away!"

Tituba tugged at Sarah's hand. "Leave the poor distracted one, missy," she pleaded. "Come meet my sweet child!"

She led Sarah to the bed. Betty Parris was small for her age, very pale and hollow-cheeked.

"Miss Elizabeth Parris, please meet—?"

"Sarah Wright." Out of habit, she curtsied. Betty smiled.

"I wish I could get up," she said hoarsely. "I have jacks we could play with."

Sarah asked, "What's wrong with you?"

The girl looked to Tituba, who looked away. "A winter malady, Papa says. A distemper of the north wind."

"They torment you!"

Abigail swooped in from behind. She shoved her face over Sarah's shoulder, leering at the bedridden girl.

"They torment you! They torment me!"

Sarah shook Abigail off. Fists knotted, she stood aside, watching Abigail drift to the other side of the room making bird noises.

A knock on the door took Tituba away. She opened it, and four new visitors barged in. Three of the girls Sarah did not know, but she recognized Betty Hubbard's tall, moon-eyed friend.

The newcomers were led by a girl about Sarah's age. She haughtily ordered Tituba about as if she were her slave. The girls surrounded Betty Parris' bed. They ignored Abigail, sitting alone by the wall, crooning to herself.

"We heard you were better today, Betty," the youngest girl said. She eyed Sarah with open suspicion. "Who's this?"

"Sarah Wright. My father and I are newly come to Salem Village."

"And where do you live?" the haughty girl asked.

"We are residing with Dr. and Goody Griggs."

"Griggs is a fool," the girl declared. Her companions gasped. "He couldn't cure frost on a windowpane!"

"He's a good man, Ann," the tall girl said. To Sarah she added, "You're staying with Betty Hubbard? How is she?"

"Unhappy," Sarah replied. Ann laughed harshly.

"Yellow birds and red, sitting on the rafters," Abigail said, raising her voice. The other girls, Ann included, were startled by her ramblings.

"Which rafters?" asked the stocky, black-haired girl.

"Right above your heads!"

They all looked up. So did Sarah. She saw nothing but thick dust on the beams.

"I see them!" cried the black-haired girl.

"No!" said Ann.

"I see them too!" Betty Parris whimpered.

One by one the girls began to weep. Sarah looked at them in amazement. Tituba, who had stayed by the door after admitting the girls, hurried to Betty. She held her close, patting her head and speaking soothing words in a language Sarah did not recognize. As the Indian woman comforted Betty, Sarah saw strange marks at the base of the girl's neck: blue and red welts, too big to be chicken pox or smallpox. Where her sleeve pulled back from her wrist, Betty had the same kind of welts on her arms, too.

Sarah backed away. Dr. Griggs would have to wait for a reply to his message.

At the door she almost ran into Goody Parris on her way in. She started to speak to Sarah, but when she heard the chorus of weeping within, she pushed past without a word. When the door shut behind Sarah, she heard screams of real terror penetrating the parsonage walls.

"All done, missy?" John Indian was there, waiting with the cart.

Sarah climbed aboard. She shivered. John offered his lap blanket. Sarah took it dumbly. It did not help. She trembled all the way home, but not from the cold.

Dr. Griggs questioned her closely when she returned. He did not seem at all concerned about his letter, or what Goody Parris did with the medicine. All he wanted to know was how Betty Parris and the other girls behaved.

"The little girl is very sick," Sarah said. She described Betty's weakness and the strange marks on her skin. "But the other one, Abigail, has lost her mind."

"Six months ago Abigail Williams was as sound as you or I," Dr. Griggs said. "Go on. You say others came to call?"

Sarah spoke of the visitors. The doctor identified the arrogant girl as Ann Putnam Junior, Mary Walcott (the black-haired girl), Mercy Lewis, and Mary Warren, who was Betty Hubbard's tall friend. Mercy Lewis, who had not said much when Sarah was there, was the blond girl with sharp features.

"That's the entire company, save for our Betty." Ephraim asked what he meant.

"The girls afflicted by witchcraft." He gave Sarah a kindly pat on the back. "I sent you to the minister's house for a special reason. I wanted to know how the girls would act around another child."

The doctor asked Sarah what she thought of what she saw. Were the girls pretending? Did their afflictions seem genuine?

"I cannot say about them all," she replied. "Betty Parris is surely sick. That girl Abigail is mad as a loon. As for the other girls . . . " She searched for the right words. "They are distracted by what they hear, I think."

The doctor's eyes widened. "You are wise for your age. Just as fever patients are separated to prevent the spread of the infection, so the bewitched should be set apart so their troubles don't worsen each other."

Dr. Griggs gave her a penny for her trouble. Ephraim hugged her as well.

That night, as the household slept, Sarah inched across the lumpy pallet to where her father slept, tired out by his work.

"Father?"

He replied at once. "What is it, lamb?"

"Why are there witches?"

Ephraim said, "Witches are misguided souls who do the Devil's bidding. They cast spells, make charms, and cause harm to innocent Christians."

This much she already knew. "But why?"

"I do not know. I'm not a learned divine." Sensing her hunger for an answer, Ephraim said, "There are people in this world who lust after power. Some want to be princes or generals, and others want to lord over their neighbors. The Devil seeks out such people and lures them into pacts. In return for the sinner's immortal soul, the Devil gives the power to work evil."

"Why does God allow it?"

"Great mercy, that's an enormous question!" At the far end of the loft, Betty Hubbard stirred in her sleep. Ephraim lowered his voice.

"God allows evil in the world to test us, I think. We have a choice of paths to take. The righteous road leads to eternal salvation in the Lord. The Devil's path leads only to death and destruction."

"What will happen to those girls?" she whispered.

"God willing, by prayer and fasting they may be saved," Ephraim said. He rolled over, away from Sarah. "Sleep now. Tomorrow comes too soon."

By morning the village was afire with word of more strange events at the Parris house. A member of the village meeting, Goodwife Sibley, had tried to help the troubled girls. She made a witch cake. Sarah heard all about it from women gossiping with Goody Griggs as they passed on their daily errands. The urine of an afflicted person (from Betty Parris, it was said) was mixed with rye meal. This was baked on the Parris hearth and fed to the family dog. Once consumed, the veil that concealed the witches was lifted. The sick girls could now see the invisible specters attacking them. More importantly, they recognized the faces of the witches hurting them.

Who were they? Two were local women Sarah did not know, Goodwife Osburn and Goodwife Good. The third accused witch was Tituba.

Sarah was astonished. She knew nothing about the first two, but her brief visit to the Parris house convinced her that Tituba loved Betty Parris dearly.

Betty Hubbard was fetching water from the spring when she heard about the witch cake and her friends' revelations. Instead of returning to the Griggs house, Betty ran away to the parsonage, where she joined Betty Parris and the other girls. The girls fell into fits, screaming and rolling on the floor, tortured by specters only they could see. Men came to Dr. Griggs' house that same afternoon, led by Thomas Putnam. His daughter Ann was

now afflicted, and in her name he had sworn out warrants for the arrest of Goody Good and Goody Osburn. Tituba was already in chains.

The delegation had not come to consult the doctor. They knew Ephraim was a former soldier. Putnam, Parris, and the others wanted Ephraim, as a man trained at arms, to serve as a constable and help round up the accused witches.

He deferred to the doctor. "I am your man these days. What say you?"

Dr. Griggs gave his permission. Ephraim donned his hat, took an oath, and accepted a spontoon from Marshal George Herrick. He was now a duly sworn constable of Essex County.

They marched away to arrest the proclaimed witches. From inside the incomplete shell of Dr. Griggs' addition, Sarah watched her father go, bearing a spear on his shoulder. She had never seen him march with such measured tread.

Goody Griggs asked her to get the water Betty Hubbard failed to provide. Once she found the spring, Sarah dipped the pitcher in the water and let it fill.

"How now?"

She looked up and saw Abe Toothaker squatting in the grass across the spring. His face was streaked with grime and his cuffs were muddier than usual. Sarah remarked on his unkempt appearance.

"I been all over the village today," he said. "Things are happening!"

"I know." Sarah hoisted the brimming pitcher out of the spring.

Abe followed her up the hill. "They say Abigail Williams tried to burn down the parsonage last night. She took brands from the fire and flung 'em about, then tried to run up the chimney!"

Sarah halted. "Why do you tell me these things?"

Abe blinked in the cold morning sunshine.

"Because I like you. Most t'other girls in the village run away or call me names. You talk to me."

Sarah suddenly felt ashamed. Abe was not a bad fellow. He was rough and ragged, but he was far friendlier than the circle of girls led by Ann Putnam.

She held out the heavy pitcher. "Carry this for me."

He did without complaint. They walked back to the house, feet swishing through the long yellow grass.

"I understand your uncle is a doctor?" Sarah said.

"He sure is. Uncle Roger's fought witches before, did I tell you?"

Sarah clasped her hands behind her back and shook her head.

"There was this bewitched boy, very sick he was, and no one could do anything for him. Then Uncle Roger told his daughter—that's my cousin Martha—to get some of the 'flicted boy's water and put it in a pot, stop it up, and put it in an oven, and stop *that* up." Abe drew a breath. "The water boiled, breaking the pot, and in the morning the witch that cast the spell on the boy was dead!"

"That's terrible!"

Abe grinned. "Not so terrible. The boy was me!"

It sounded to Sarah that Dr. Toothaker and Cousin Martha were using witchcraft to fight witchcraft, hardly a Christian thing to do. Since Abe's life was saved by the deed, she said nothing.

"Why do you think there are witches, Abe?"

Abe set the pitcher down in the grass. "There's good people in the world, and bad people," he said. "Just like there's God and His angels, and the Devil and his demons. If that's so, why shouldn't there be witches, too?"

Abe hoisted the jug and started down the hill. Sarah followed. Abe left her at the Griggs doorstep. Goody Griggs did not like him, he said, calling him a "dirty rascal," among other things.

Ephraim did not come home until very late. Dr. Griggs was away all afternoon. Sarah did her best to help around the house, but Goody Griggs was upset by the events. She sat and fretted, jabbing herself every time she turned to her needlework. Eventually, she gave up and sat close to the fire, reading her psalms.

Night fell on the woman and the girl, alone in the half-finished house. Sarah went to bring in firewood. Despite the recent thaw, the night was icy and windswept. The moon rose behind Leach's Hill, casting a jaundiced glow over the land.

Bands of clouds, combed by the wind, crossed the moon's face, periodically plunging everything into sudden darkness.

The first time this happened, Sarah was five steps from the woodpile. She halted, blind. When the moon emerged again, it brought to life a hundred dancing shadows: tree limbs shaken by the wind, fence posts and their staggered rails, and the quick-moving clouds. A dog howled far away. Sarah drew her cloak tight at her throat.

A rectangle of warm light fell on Sarah's back.

"Child, are you lost?" Goody Griggs called. Sarah heaped cordwood in her arms and hurried back.

The doctor returned soon after. His mood was grim. More afflictions had come to the village. Ann Putnam's mother, Ann Senior, was under spectral attack. The victims had identified new witches.

The doctor and his wife turned in. Sarah remained at the hearth, waiting for her father. The fire died to a heap of glowing coals. The embers glowed red as blood. Abe told her witches used blood as a sacrament, in horrible parody of the Lord's Holy Communion. Their names were inscribed in the Devil's book in blood.

Sarah heard the latch lift. Thinking it was her father, she tried to rise to greet him. Her legs would not move. Surprised, she tried again. She could not move her arms or legs at all.

The person entering the Griggs house drifted into her line of sight.

"Who are you?" Sarah wanted to say. No words escaped her lips. The strange visitor glided closer. Sarah's heart beat faster. Slowly, the stranger bent down. Its face was ghostly white, framed by a dark cowl. The thing's eyes were black. Not in the center, like a person's eyes, but black from corner to corner, like a beast's.

"God save me!"

When the words burst from her lips, Sarah snapped upright. Her hand almost went in the fire. She whirled about wildly, but the specter was gone. Seeing a shadowed figure standing by the door, she uttered a loud cry and threw up her hands to ward off the apparition.

Ephraim walked into the circle of firelight. He removed his hat and propped his spontoon against the wall.

"It's me, child. Are you well?"

She did not reply, but ran to him and threw her arms around his neck.

chapter six

Before Justice

Reverend Parris invited ministers from nearby churches to help him with the afflicted. They prayed, and they fasted, but the torments continued. Of the original group of girls, only Betty Parris was sent away to escape the terror. The others remained together, stricken by unseen enemies.

This much Ephraim reported after he returned from rounding up two accused witches, Sarah Osburn and Sarah Good. Two judges from Salem Town were due to arrive today to examine them and Tituba on charges of witchcraft. It was the first of March 1692.

Sarah walked with her father to court. Ephraim bore the spontoon on his shoulder. Thomas Putnam offered him a helmet, but Ephraim declined. He had worn an iron pot too long in the King's service to ever want to wear one again.

People streamed into the village from the outlying farms. The judges, Mr. Hathorne and Mr. Corwin, were due to hold court at Nathaniel Ingersoll's Ordinary, the main tavern in the village.

"Watch Good," Ephraim said as they neared the Ordinary. "The Indian woman is too afraid to make trouble, and Goody Osburn is a poor cripple. Good is a desperate character." He shook his head. "Mark her well."

The crowd parted for Ephraim. Sarah kept close behind him. She spotted Abe Toothaker perched on a fence post, trying to see over the crowd. He waved to Sarah. She waved back, strangely pleased to see him.

The door to Ingersoll's tavern was blocked by a group of important-looking men. They wore city clothes: black boots, buffed hats, and well-tailored cloaks. In the center of the group were the two stern-looking magistrates, John Hathorne and Jonathan Corwin. Everyone listened attentively when they spoke. Judge Hathorne dominated the conversation despite his rather high-pitched voice.

"The hall is plainly too small," he was saying. "We can't conduct the King's affairs with witnesses and spectators hanging from the rafters like roosting chickens!"

"Turn the rabble away," Judge Corwin suggested.

The marshal spoke up: "You can't force these people to go. They will riot."

"What tumult! Is there another place to go?" Hathorne said.

Ephraim stepped forward. "Your Worship! May I suggest the meetinghouse? It is larger than the tavern."

"Meetinghouse? Is Reverend Parris here?" Hathorne snapped.

Parris shouldered through the crowd. "I am here, Your Worship."

"We will hold court in your meetinghouse," Hathorne said briskly. "Is it agreed?"

Reverend Parris had little choice. He led the way. The judges and their entourage followed. Marshal Herrick stopped Ephraim and some other men-at-arms.

"Retrieve the prisoners from the watch house," he said. "Be quick!"

Sarah was able to squeeze into the meetinghouse behind the judges. Once inside she made her way to the far side of the room, facing the door.

The people of Salem Village crowded in while tables and chairs were arranged below the pulpit to create the judges' bench. There was not room for everyone. People pressed in around the open door and windows, eager to hear everything.

Sarah glimpsed Abe at the door. He wanted to get in, but no one would yield to him. Sarah dared call, "Abe! Over here!" Hearing the boy beckoned, men and women at the door allowed Abe through. He darted between the benches and slid against the wall at Sarah's side, grinning gratefully.

"Hear ye, hear ye, the magistrates' court for the County of Essex in the Province of Massachusetts Bay is now in session!" chanted the bailiff. Everyone stood up. The room fell quiet.

"The honorable John Hathorne and the honorable Jonathan Corwin, presiding. God Save the King! God Save the Queen!"

The judges sat down. A man whose name Sarah heard was Ezekiel Cheever sat at a table on the judges' left. He dipped a quill into an inkwell and began to write down what was said.

"Be seated," Judge Hathorne said. Those few lucky enough to have a bench did so. Most of the crowd remained on their feet.

"Are the afflicted ones present?" Hathorne asked.

"They have been summoned, Your Honor," the marshal said.

"Are the prisoners present?"

"They are being fetched from jail, sir."

Hathorne scowled. "They would make us wait for them? This is bad process!"

The girls, led by Abigail Williams, appeared at the meetinghouse door. The bailiff led them in. One by one they passed between the judges' table and the onlookers, taking seats on the front bench, which had been reserved for them. They looked perfectly normal. Abigail Williams peeked around at all the people present. The younger Ann Putnam sat primly beside her, studiously avoiding everyone's gaze. Four young women filed in beside the younger girls. Betty Hubbard slumped on the bench, head down, trying not to be seen. Mercy Lewis, who had a reputation of being a saucy creature, carefully smoothed her dress, her apron, and her cap. Mary Warren looked pale and strained. Sixteen-year-old Mary Walcott sniffled, dabbing at her nose with a scrap of cloth.

When the afflicted girls were seated, a very prolonged murmuring filled the room, and everyone whispered, stared, or pointed. Mary Walcott began sobbing.

Reverend Parris was asked to lead the assembly in prayer. He did, quoting from Psalm 18: "For thou wilt save the afflicted people, but will bring down high looks, For thou wilt light my candle: the Lord my God will enlighten my darkness."

At last, the constables arrived with the accused. Judge Hathorne rapped his knuckles on the table to quiet the room. Marshal Herrick brought in Tituba in chains. Next, two men supported a bowed, crippled woman between them. Abe whispered that she was Sarah Osburn. Ephraim Wright followed, leading a defiant-looking woman with shackles on her wrists. This was Sarah Good. Sarah was startled to recognize the pipe-smoking beggar woman she had seen tramping the lanes of Salem Village.

The accused were held together on Hathorne's right, in full view of the crowd. Hathorne had the indictments read. Sarah heard a lot of words she did not understand, whereas and wherefore, and bits of foreign terms she guessed were Latin. The gist of it was that the three women were accused of using witchcraft to harm the afflicted. Since children were not allowed to bring charges on their own, the fathers or male kinsmen of the girls officially lodged the complaints.

Tituba and Sarah Osburn were taken out so that Sarah Good could be examined first.

Hathorne did not waste any time. He demanded, "Sarah Good, what evil spirit have you familiarity with?"

The gray-eyed woman, hair askew and clothes long soiled, snapped back, "None!"

"Have you made no contracts with the Devil?"

"No!"

"Why do you hurt these children?"

She folded her arms. "I do not hurt them. I scorn it!"

Hathorne pressed on. "Who do you employ then to do it?"

"Nobody. Do I look like I have money to employ anyone?"

There were a few chuckles. Hathorne glowered at the crowd, and the laughter ceased.

"What creature do you employ then?"

"No creature. I am falsely accused."

"Why did you go muttering from Mr. Parris' house?"

"I did not mutter." She looked away, cheeks coloring. "I thanked him for what he gave my child."

Sarah Good had a five-year-old daughter, Dorcas, and a baby still young enough to be nursing. Because she had fallen on hard times, Sarah Good roamed the countryside, begging for food or money for her children.

Judge Hathorne turned to the afflicted women and girls. "Is this one of the persons who hurt you?"

With nods or curt yesses, Betty Hubbard and her companions identified Sarah Good as one of their tormentors.

When it was Ann Putnam's turn, she declared loudly, "Sarah Good pinched me most grievously, choked me, and burned me, trying to force me to write my name in the Devil's book!"

When she was finished, Abigail Williams let out a shrill, long laugh. She flung her head from side to side so violently her cap flew off and her hair became a mad tangle. Mercy Lewis fell off the bench face-first and rolled on the floor, moaning. Like birds leaving a clothesline, one by one the other girls collapsed on the floor. Mary Warren made weird barking sounds. Betty Hubbard drooled and clawed the air. Ann Putnam Junior resisted for a time. Then her chin dropped to her chest. She shivered, then leaped to her feet, roaring like a beast. Her father and some other men moved in to restrain her. She screamed wild words and swung her fists, fighting invisible foes.

Sarah clutched Abe's hand. Wincing, he pried her fingers loose. Abigail Williams spotted them in the crowd and gaped at them. She stuck out her tongue. More and more of it came out until it seemed to Sarah that a serpent was escaping from the poor girl's mouth. She shut her eyes.

Over the uproar, Judge Hathorne continued to question Sarah Good.

"Do you not see now what you have done? Why do you not tell us the truth? Why do you thus torment these poor children?"

Sarah opened her eyes when she heard Goody Good reply again, "I employ nobody. I scorn it!"

Her voice was full of disgust. Everyone else in the meetinghouse was stricken with horror, pity, or both, but not Sarah Good. She beheld the afflicted with utter contempt.

"How come they thus tormented?" the judge said.

"How do I know? You brought others here. Why blame me? Maybe the others are doing it."

"Which one?" Hathorne said sharply. "Who was it, then, that tormented the children?"

Sarah Good slowly unfolded her arms. "Maybe it was Osburn . . . "

Sensing uncertainty, Hathorne kept after her: Why did she go away from people's houses muttering? What did it mean? Was she uttering curses?

"I was saying my Commandments. I may say the Commandments, I hope."

Hathorne pressed her to name the Commandment she said. Sarah Good shifted from one foot to the other, rolling her empty clay pipe between her fingers.

"If I must tell you, I will tell. It was a psalm," she said. She stammered for the first time, reciting, "'A poor woman cries, and the Lord hears her, saving her from trouble.'"

Sarah Wright recognized the verse she meant to say. It was from Psalm 34: "This poor man cried, and the Lord heard him, and saved him from his troubles."

Hathorne sat back. He produced a sheet of paper half covered with writing.

"I have here a statement made by your husband, William Good. In it he says he fears you are a witch, or will be one quickly."

"You cannot hold against me what fools say!" Sarah Good said.

"He says, 'I may say with tears, that she is an enemy to all good.' Why would a husband say this of his wife?"

"He is a worthless layabout. He wishes to be rid of me."

Judge Corwin, who had said nothing during the examination, leaned close and muttered something in his colleague's ear. All this time the afflicted girls had been screaming and contorting.

At Hathorne's direction, chains were put on Sarah Good's ankles, and two sturdy constables took hold of her arms. One by one the tormented girls fell silent.

"Now that you are restrained, you cannot harm them. Is that not so?" Hathorne said.

"I have done nothing but speak to Your Worship," she replied. "If you're looking for a witch, question Osburn."

"That is what I intend. Take her out."

Sarah Good went out as defiantly as she had come in. Murmurs of "black-hearted witch" followed her out. She dug in her heels and turned to the crowd. Glaring fiercely, Sarah Good dared anyone to speak to her face. No one did.

Ephraim gave her a firm push. "Come along," he said calmly. She went out, still smoldering with resentment.

"She must be a witch!" Abe said under his breath.

She was certainly bad-tempered. Sarah wondered if that came from selling her soul to the Devil, or from being reduced to beggary.

Lame in both legs, Sarah Osburn had to be carried in. Judge Hathorne asked her to look upon the afflicted girls. No sooner had their eyes met than fresh madness overcame the girls. Sarah Osburn's mouth fell open in astonishment as the victims rolled and arched their backs, clawed at phantoms, screeched wildly, howled, and screamed.

"What evil spirit have you familiarity with?" said the judge over the din.

"None," answered Goody Osburn, voice trembling.

"Have you made no contract with the Devil?"

"No. I never saw the Devil in my life." She denied ever employing any demons to hurt the children. Hathorne changed his approach.

"What familiarity have you with Sarah Good?"

"None. I had none, only to say 'How do you do?' I do not know her by name."

Hathorne peered down his long nose at her. "Sarah Good saith that it was you that hurt the children. How do you answer that?"

Sarah Osburn scratched the flannel bands wrapped around her head for warmth. "Maybe—maybe the Devil goes about in my likeness to do harm?"

Hathorne polled the girls, some of whom had come out of their fits.

"Does this woman hurt you?"

Abigail and Ann affirmed that she did. Mercy Lewis offered that Sarah Osburn was not a witch, but bewitched herself. Betty Hubbard loudly declared that the specter of Sarah Osburn had burned her with a hot brand, slapped her, and pulled her hair so hard a clump came out with bloody roots. Judge Corwin ordered Betty examined for such an injury. Women from the audience looked over Betty and found nothing. Her wounds were spectral rather than physical, the judges decided.

Hathorne tried to test Goody Osburn's Christian character. It was reported, he said, that Goody Osburn had not been to meeting in over a year.

The frail woman rubbed a hand down her thigh. "I have been ill, Your Worship, and could not come to meeting."

She was not combative like Sarah Good, but Goody Osburn would not admit any guilt. She was dismissed back to jail. Coughing into a rag, she was carried out.

Tituba was called next. The Indian woman entered, heavily shackled. She was the first of the accused witches who looked truly frightened.

"Tituba," Hathorne began, "what evil spirit have you familiarity with?"

"None, Your Worship," she said softly. Hathorne went through the same list of questions he asked Good and Osburn.

Finally, he said, "Who hurts these children?"

"The Devil, for aught I know."

Corwin and Hathorne exchanged glances. Judge Corwin said, "Did you ever see the Devil?"

Tituba took a deep breath. There was sweat on her dark brow, enough to stain the scarf around her head.

"The Devil came to me, and bid me serve him."

Gasps could be heard all around the room. Prompted by the triumphant judges, Tituba described the society of witches infesting Salem Village. She knew of four others, two of whom were Good and Osburn. She did not know the remaining two. Their leader was "a tall man from Boston." The witches pressured Tituba to join them and hurt the children. They haunted her night and day, appearing as black dogs, or monstrous pigs, and sometimes as birds or cats. Always they commanded the slave woman to hurt the children or be killed herself. Worn down and terrified, Tituba allowed her spectral form to go forth and torment Abigail, Ann, and the others.

"But I will hurt them no more," Tituba vowed.

"This tall man from Boston—did you meet him?" Hathorne asked.

"He came to me and said, 'Serve me!' He was a tall man, dressed in black clothes, with white hair and—"

She let her words hang so long Judge Hathorne prompted her to go on.

"He had a yellow bird on his shoulder."

Sarah shivered. Abigail Williams had long raved about invisible yellow birds.

The tall man from Boston—perhaps the Devil in person— promised Tituba pretty things if she served him. If she refused, a terrible fate awaited her.

"What pretty things?" the judge wanted to know. Tituba shrugged. From her vantage point, Sarah saw a great welt under the Indian woman's collar when she made the gesture. Sarah knew the marks of a lash when she saw them.

A host of evil spirits haunted Tituba. Yellow and red birds, black cats, and more monstrous things: "a thing with a head like a woman, with two legs and wings."

Abigail Williams, who had been listening quietly, jumped up on the bench and cried, "I did see that creature at Mr. Parris' house, warming itself by the fire! When I called out to it, it turned into Goody Osburn!"

"Who was it that attacked Elizabeth Hubbard last Saturday?" Hathorne said, after consulting his notes.

"Sarah Good set a wolf on her," Tituba said.

At that, Betty Hubbard began trembling violently. Still standing on the bench, Abigail shouted, "There is the wolf again! It bites Betty!"

Betty fell to the floor, clutching her leg and screaming. Mary Walcott and Mary Warren scrambled away, fleeing the spectral beast. Ann Putnam Junior laughed maniacally and pointed at the awful sight.

"Do you see who torments these children now?" said Hathorne, rising to his feet.

"I am blind now. I cannot see," Tituba said.

She testified no more. When the constables came to escort her back to jail, Tituba fell to the floor in fits. They carried her out while she raved that yellow birds were drinking her blood.

Sarah Good's spirit continued to harass the afflicted girls, Betty Hubbard in particular. Ephraim was told that the accused witch had escaped from Marshal Herrick's house where she was being held. She shed her shoes and stockings (in the middle of a New England winter) and tiptoed away with her baby in her arms. Afraid for her baby's life in the cold, she soon returned.

The three accused witches were transferred to jail in Salem Town. For a while the tormented girls got better, then new witches turned up to torture them. The specter of Dorcas Good, Sarah Good's five-year-old daughter, bit and choked Ann Putnam Junior. Others claimed they were attacked by the specter of Martha Cory. Unlike the slave Tituba, the crippled Osburn, or the beggar Sarah Good, Goody Cory was a member of the Salem Village meeting. Goody Cory met the accusation of witchcraft even more scornfully than Sarah Good did. She was a gospel woman, she declared. Her protests of innocence caused worse fits among the bewitched, and Goody Cory was arrested. Then the afflicted claimed a new witch appeared to torment them: Rebecca Nurse, an elderly lady of pious reputation.

Dr. and Goody Griggs were stunned by this accusation. Not only was Rebecca Nurse known as a gentle Christian, but her chief accusers, Ann Putnam mother and daughter, had long been at odds with the Nurse family. They had many disputes over the ownership of land between their farms.

"It cannot be true," Goody Griggs said. "The Devil is deceiving the poor afflicted ones!" Nevertheless, Ephraim was called to round up the new suspects.

Because Betty Hubbard was spending so much time at the Parris house, praying and fasting with Reverend Parris and his colleagues from surrounding towns—Mr. Hale of Beverly, Mr. Noyes of Salem Town, and old Reverend Higginson, also of Salem—much of her work fell to Sarah Wright. Sarah fetched water and went to the village to buy eggs or barter for nails for the doctor.

The arrests of suspected witches did not end the trouble. Whenever accused witches were taken into custody, new ones were seen by the tormented. The afflicted girls had visions every day, and their suffering was spreading. People outside the original group of young girls fell ill to the witchcraft infesting Essex County.

Ann Putnam's mother was stricken, along with goodwives Bathshua Pope and Sarah Bibber. Sarah Wright saw them at the questioning of Goody Nurse. Goody Pope was a plump and pleasant-looking lady. Goody Bibber had a face like a terrier, with a long nose, a sharp chin, and close-set eyes. Ann Putnam Senior looked a lot like her daughter—same fair hair, same haughty manner. Her pride vanished when the evil took hold of her. Mother Ann screeched and growled as horribly as her daughter. Sarah had never heard such sounds from a woman's lips.

Goodwife Nurse made a far better impression. At seventy, she was white-haired and had the gentle manner of a Godly woman. Even Judge Hathorne was perplexed at having such a sincere Christian accused of witchcraft. Those who had gone before—Sarah Good, Osburn, even church member Martha Cory—had all demonstrated malice, skepticism, and bad faith before the court. Rebecca Nurse did none of these things.

"I can say before my eternal Father I am innocent, and God will clear my innocence," said Goody Nurse, standing before the magistrates.

Hathorne replied, "I pray God clear you if you be innocent, and if you be guilty discover you."

He suggested that the Devil might have made Rebecca Nurse a witch without her knowledge. This struck Sarah Wright as a peculiar thing to say. How could anyone become a servant of the Devil without consenting to do so? Goody Nurse was puzzled, too, and denied it. Confronted by the agonies of the afflicted as well as their accusation, she simply said, "I cannot tell what to think of it." In the end she fell back on the defense Sarah Osburn had first suggested.

"I cannot help it," Goody Nurse said. "The Devil may appear in my shape."

Whatever doubts were raised by the charges against Rebecca Nurse were dispelled by the testimony of Dorcas Good. Dorcas was five years old. She looked like a wild thing in her patched and dirty clothes, hair a tangle. Sarah and her father talked about her over supper that night.

Dr. Griggs and his wife were out. There were reports of more bewitched people in the outlying parts of the village. The doctor had gone to examine them. It was like an epidemic, only an epidemic of evil instead of disease. Goody Griggs had gone along to help, psalm book clasped firmly in her hands.

Alone in the house, the Wrights ate a meager supper of pottage.

"That child needs a bath and a month of good meals," Ephraim said later. Instead they had paraded Dorcas in front of the packed meetinghouse where the afflicted ones ranted and roared. Faced with that, what did Dorcas Good do? She confessed.

"Did you bite these girls?" Judge Hathorne had asked.

"Yes, sir," the child said.

"Why?"

"My mother told me to."

Everyone in the court had seen the small sets of teeth marks on the arms and necks of the afflicted, marks too small to have been made by anyone but a child.

"What else does your mother tell you to do?" prompted the judge.

"To care for my creature."

"A familiar spirit?" asked Hathorne.

"Yes," said Dorcas gravely. "It is a snake. It bites my finger here and sucks out blood."

There was a red mark on the girl's finger, Ephraim said. She was covered with them. They were probably fleabites, her father said.

Sitting in the firelight at the Griggses' table, Sarah was horrified. "They cannot believe that little girl is a witch!"

"She sits in jail right now."

She did not know what to think. It was easy to accept that an Indian woman like Tituba had knowledge of the Devil. Her people worshipped demons and devils, and however Christian she pretended to be, the Devil never forgot his own. Sarah Osburn seemed addled by age and disease, but Sarah Good was as hateful and malevolent as a witch should be. Martha Cory, it was said, had unnatural knowledge of things said far away from her. But who could believe kindly old Rebecca Nurse or pathetic Dorcas Good were in league with the Devil?

She sought out Abe Toothaker the next day. She found him skipping stones in the Frost Fish River, down the hill from Dr. Griggs' house.

"Do you think all those people accused of witchcraft are guilty, Abe?"

Another missile streaked from his hand. "I do."

"What makes you so sure?"

"The Devil is always after our souls," the boy said, studying his latest trajectory. "We are all weak sinners. That's what Mr. Parris says. Stands to reason some weak sinners would take the Devil's offer and serve him."

"Even a five-year-old girl?" Sarah asked.

"Why not? Her mother's a witch. Children grow up the way their folks intend." Abe turned away from the water, skinning the sleeves back from his arms. "I seen the bite marks on Mary Warren's arms. They were little, like a little child made them, and there was gaps in the marks like the gaps in Dorcas' teeth."

Sarah sighed and sat down in the grass.

"Why would honest Christians trade their immortal soul to the Evil One for power over their neighbors? It sounds like a bad bargain to me!"

Abe reclined beside her, pulling the brim of his hat down to shade his eyes.

"Some folks hasn't got any other choice. I mean, if you were old and weak, or poor and starving, might you be tempted?"

"No. Would you be, Absalom Toothaker?"

"Not me. There's lots of ways to make your way in the world. You don't have to be a saint or a witch, just use your head. That's what my uncle Roger does."

Sarah smiled. "You admire your uncle."

"He's a great man."

Stretched out in the grass, Abe soon fell asleep. Sarah left him there, loose stones spilling from his pockets onto the greening turf.

She walked home through unmown fields. When she and her father had arrived in Salem Village, she could tell people were afraid of something. She thought it was the Indians or the French. Now the threat had a name—*witchcraft*—and the fear had grown worse. When Sarah went on her errands for Goody Griggs, she often had to knock six or eight times on farmhouse doors before anyone would answer. Neighbor looked on neighbor with suspicion, and there was no comfort anywhere, not even in God's meetinghouse. If pillars of the church like Rebecca Nurse could be witches, then no one could be trusted.

chapter seven

The Invisible World

Spring arrived in Essex County, but even as trees grew green and fields were plowed, the stain of witchcraft spread wider and wider. More people fell under the evil hand, including Tituba's man, John Indian. Whole families came under suspicion: the Proctors, husband and wife, were accused; Martha and Giles Cory; and the two sisters of Rebecca Nurse. Every new arrest provoked more fits and more spectral visitations. There seemed to be no end to the Devil's disciples.

The visions of the afflicted grew more alarming. Abigail Williams beheld a great witch meeting in Reverend Parris' pasture. Forty witches turned out, led by Sarah Good and Sarah Cloyse, one of Rebecca Nurse's sisters. Blood taken from the tortured girls of Salem Village was shared among the witches as a sacrament. Red bread was eaten. Mary Walcott, who was having so many seizures she could barely speak, supported Abigail's claim.

Spring also brought Sarah Wright new burdens. Goody Griggs' specter was seen by a local man in the company of the accused witches. Goody Griggs was not arrested, as the doctor was able to show that her accuser was prone to epilepsy and owed Dr. Griggs money for past treatments. Goody Griggs was so frightened by the accusation that she did not go out for eight days. She asked Sarah to fetch, trade, and do all her errands. It was too much for a twelve-year-old on foot, so Dr. Griggs arranged for Sarah to have the use of a neighbor's pony.

On the fourth day of Goody Griggs' retreat, Sarah was riding through the village. She passed the meetinghouse, empty since the court was not in session. She rounded the bend in the road by Ingersoll's tavern, and whom should she encounter but Ann Putnam Junior, Abigail Williams, Mary Warren, Mercy Lewis, Mary Walcott, and Betty Hubbard, walking past in single file. Young Ann ignored her, as she often snubbed those she considered inferior, but Abigail skipped out in front of the pony. Sarah drew back the reins, and the pony, named Tassel, shuffled to stop.

"Give way," she said. "I have places I must go."

Abigail took hold of the bridle and stared into Tassel's brown eyes. "What evil spirit have you familiarity with?" she intoned, imitating Judge Hathorne.

Tassel stared placidly back. Mary Walcott giggled. That was natural enough, but she could not stop. She kept giggling until Ann Putnam doubled back and slapped her.

"Stop it, Ann," Mary Warren said.

"We've no time to waste on common vagabonds," Ann replied. "Take hold of yourself, Mary. Let go the bridle, Abby."

Abigail continued to gaze into the pony's unblinking eye. "You are now in the hands of authority! Confess you are a servant of the Old Snake!"

Ann tried to drag Abigail aside. To her astonishment, Abigail shoved her into Mercy and Mary Warren.

"I know you, Sarah Wright," Abigail said, stroking the pony's blunt nose. "The invisible world is plain to me. I see you in the Eastward."

"Abigail—!" Mary Warren warned. Betty Hubbard began to sob.

It was no secret she and her father came to the village from Maine. Sarah tugged at the reins, but Abigail held fast to the pony's bridle.

"You came without your brother or your mother. Your brother's name was . . . " Abigail closed her eyes. "Simon, not called Peter." She smiled and opened them again. "Your mother was Mary."

"Out of my way," Sarah repeated, growing angry.

"I see what happened to them. Indians came. Before dawn. They hid in the cornfield and took your brother first when he went to milk the cow. They missed your father because he went down to the river to fish. Your mother went to find your brother, and the braves seized her like this!"

Abigail threw her arms behind her back, fists clenched.

"For pity's sake, Abby! Say no more!" Mary Warren said. The Walcott girl giggled again.

"They were going to carry her off, but your father returned. Not wanting to give their captives back, they cut her throat and your brother's, too, with a—" Abigail let go of the bridle. She looked up at Sarah.

"With a sickle."

The next thing Sarah knew, she was off the pony. She grabbed Abigail by the apron and drove her backward, nose to nose. The girls lost their footing and tumbled to the ground with Sarah on top.

"Liar! You can't know that!" Sarah cried.

Strong hands dragged her off the unresisting Abigail. Sarah thought the older girls had intervened, but it was Reverend Parris and Mr. Ingersoll, the tavern keeper.

Tears streamed down Sarah's face. Despite the awful dreams, she had never spoken of the fate of her mother and brother, not even to her father. How did mad Abigail Williams know the truth?

Reverend Parris asked Sarah and Abigail why they were fighting. Sarah was too upset to answer. Abigail got up, covered in the dust of the road. Her nose was bleeding.

"I-I don't know . . . who's fighting, Uncle Samuel?" The mocking tone was gone from her voice and manner.

"Why, you and this child!" Parris said.

Nathaniel Ingersoll brought Tassel forward. He helped Sarah mount and gave her the reins.

"Go about your business, girl. There's enough trouble in the village," Ingersoll said. "Do not add to it."

The other girls quickly departed, Betty Hubbard weeping and Mary Walcott giggling. Reverend Parris hovered over Abigail, brushing the dust from her clothes and smoothing her hair. Abigail said nothing, but stood before him, dazed. He was kneeling, and his niece was able to peer over his shoulder as Sarah rode away.

Sarah looked back. She does not remember what she said, Sarah thought, seeing Abigail's blank eyes.

Down the road, Sarah stopped by a brook. She brought handfuls of water to her face and let the chill of it cut through her simmering rage. Sitting back on her feet, she looked across the fields, neatly plowed for spring planting. Despite the outward appearance of order, Salem Village did not look like a proper farm community. The fields were empty. When the morning plowing was done, all work ceased. No children played in the clear sunlight. Cattle and poultry were locked in pens and barns so the Evil Eye could not claim them. Winter had gone, but cold silence still gripped the village.

One thought haunted her: If Abigail really could see the invisible world of ghosts and spirits, then her revelations about the witches she saw could be accurate, too.

She heard bright, off-key whistling. Who else would it be but Abe Toothaker, carrying a willow pole on his shoulder? He had been fishing in some pond, by the look of him.

"Abe!" she called, springing to her feet. The boy shaded his eyes. He changed direction to meet her.

"You have a horse?" Abe asked, delighted.

"It is borrowed. I am doing some errands for Goody Griggs."

They rode double on Tassel, and Sarah's chores passed quickly now that she had company. It was barely noon when they returned to the Griggs house. Ephraim was sawing timber when he spotted Sarah and Abe.

Sarah got down and led the pony to where her father worked.

"Father, this is Absalom Toothaker," she said.

From the pony, Abe tugged a forelock.

"How do y'do, sir," he said.

"I recall meeting Goodman Toothaker before," Ephraim said. Abe grinned at being addressed like a grown-up. "Are you done with your labors?"

Sarah pointed to the sack hanging heavily from the saddle.

"You'd best take it in. Goody Griggs awaits."

When Sarah returned, she found her father and Abe speaking gravely. The topic was witchcraft.

"So Goodwife Bishop has been accused?" Ephraim asked. Abe nodded. "She's a cozener, I'll grant, but a witch? Who has accused her?"

"All the afflicted ones, especially the grown ladies, and Reverend Parris' man, John Indian."

Sarah remembered Bridget Bishop quite well. She was the colorfully dressed woman who ran her home as a tavern.

Her father had paid a high price for Bridget's hospitality, then returned the favor by exposing her crooked shovel-board game.

"Goody Bishop's been counted a witch before," Abe said. "Everybody says she bewitched her first husband, Goodman Wasslebee, to death."

Ephraim looked weary. More arrests meant more constabulary work for him. Working for Dr. Griggs and Essex County was wearing him out.

"Ask him," muttered Abe.

"I will, I will," Sarah hissed.

"Ask me what?"

On the ride back from her errands, Sarah and Abe had hatched a plot. She blurted, "I want to go to Salem, Father."

Ephraim's eyebrows rose. "Why?"

"To see the witches in jail!" Abe said.

Ephraim frowned. "Ogling the unfortunate is not seemly."

Sarah caught his arm. "Please, Father, it's not a spectacle I want to see. It's that little girl, Dorcas. She's only five. I want to see if she is well."

His expression instantly changed. "That is a gentle notion," he said. "You may go, but only when the sheriff next asks me to take or collect a prisoner."

Ephraim went back to his saw. Abe departed, bubbling with anticipation. He made Sarah promise not to forget him when it came time to go to Salem.

When Abe was gone, Sarah wove her way through the unfinished walls of Dr. Griggs' addition. Her father struggled to fit a heavy timber brace.

"Speak," he said. He always knew when Sarah was troubled. She told him of her encounter with Abigail Williams and the afflicted girls.

"Stay away from them," he said sternly. Ephraim put his shoulder to the timber and heaved. It slid into place. "They are dangerous."

"But how did Abigail know—?"

"About your mother and Simon?" Sarah nodded mutely. "I told Dr. Griggs and Marshal Herrick. Either of them may have repeated the story in the girls' hearing."

Reassuring in one way, her father's information troubled her in another. If Abigail was dressing up gossip as a revelation from the invisible world, how could they believe her claims of spectral attacks by witches? She said as much to her father.

"That, lamb, is the question."

Sarah circled around the post to see his face better.

"Do you believe what the afflicted ones say?"

Ephraim picked up a mallet and began banging the brace into position. He said, "I believe there are witches. Folk have confessed as such here and in the past. Whether their spirits can be seen in the air, tormenting innocent people . . . " He gave the beam a last mighty blow. "I pray every night the afflicted ones see and speak the truth."

Bridget Bishop was brought before the magistrates soon after. Ephraim and Sarah were in court when Goody Bishop was examined.

Judge Hathorne was especially severe that day. Earlier, Mary Warren had recanted her testimony, declaring, "The afflicted persons did dissemble"—that is, they lied about seeing spectral witches. Questioned on that point, Mary broke down when the other girls accused her of invisibly torturing them. She collapsed in court, had severe seizures, and had to be removed to maintain order. The judge was in a grim mood by the time he faced the notorious Bridget Bishop.

"You stand charged with sundry acts of witchcraft, committed upon the bodies of Mercy Lewis, Ann Putnam, and others," he began in a low, tense voice.

"I am innocent. I know nothing of it. I have done no witchcraft," Goody Bishop replied.

To the afflicted group, Hathorne said, "Look upon this woman and see if this be the woman that you have seen hurting you."

The victims, now including adult women and John Indian, cried out that she was hurting them even as he spoke.

"What do you say now that they charge you to your face?" the judge asked. His face stood out white as marble against his black coat.

"I never did hurt them in my life!" Bridget declared. "In my life I did never see those persons before. I am as innocent as a child unborn!"

Sarah heard several people mutter that Goody Bishop was lying. No one in Salem Village could claim not to know the Putnam family, and anyone who frequented Ingersoll's tavern would know John Indian and Abigail Williams.

Judge Hathorne launched into a series of questions about Bridget Bishop's clothes. Were they torn anywhere? She was puzzled by the query. The bailiffs examined her skirt and found two parallel tears in the back.

Jonathan Walcott, father of the terrified Mary Walcott, testified that Mary had seen the apparition of Bridget Bishop in his house while having a horrible fit. At her direction, Walcott had swung his sheathed sword at the empty air, trying to strike the phantom. Mary claimed his sword snagged on Bridget Bishop's dress—and there were two rents in the fabric, such as might have been made by a covered blade.

"Goody Bishop, what contract have you made with the Devil?" Hathorne demanded.

"I have made no contract with the Devil. I never saw him in my life!"

They went back and forth like this, Hathorne accusing and Bishop denying. Both raised their voices until Judge Corwin had a quiet word with his fellow judge. Hathorne listened, nodded, then coolly asked, "What do you say about these horrible acts of witchcraft you see here?"

Not understanding his change in tactics, Goody Bishop said defiantly, "I know nothing of it. I do not know if there even are any witches, or no."

Ephraim gave Sarah's hand a warning squeeze.

"Have you not heard? Some have confessed to their witchcraft," Judge Corwin said calmly.

"I have not heard," Bridget answered.

Two farmers who frequented Goody Bishop's makeshift tavern promptly testified that they had conversations with her about the doings of the court, including the confessions of Tituba and Dorcas Good.

"Enter a charge of perjury against the defendant," Hathorne ordered.

Goody Bishop loudly protested. Her cries were immediately drowned out by the screams and thrashing of the afflicted. Hathorne demanded quiet, but the fits went on with redoubled fury. Not until Bridget Bishop was removed in irons did the afflicted ones calm down.

Ephraim ushered Sarah from the court. "She's lying her way into a noose," he said, shaking his head.

"Is she a witch?" asked Sarah.

"I know not. She is a liar, that's certain, and if she doesn't change her answers, she's going to end up on the gallows."

Other testimony was given against Bridget Bishop besides the ravings of the tormented. For years she had quarreled with her neighbors, and her neighbors had suffered from strange illnesses, bad luck, and premature death. Worst of all, during renovations to a house Bridget Bishop had lived in, rag dolls pierced with pins were found buried in a cellar wall. A chill of fear went through the courtroom when this evidence was presented. Image magic was the most dreaded form of witchcraft, and here was plain evidence of it.

The judges condemned Bridget Bishop to death for practicing witchcraft. Her conviction preceded everyone else accused of the crime, even the much feared Sarah Good.

Four stout constables were recruited to take Goody Bishop to jail. Ephraim was one of them. A horse, paid for by the county, was his to ride to Salem and back. He accepted the task on one condition.

"I want my daughter, Sarah, to accompany me."

Marshal Herrick puffed his pipe and considered. "So long as she does not impair the execution of your duties, it is well with me," he said. Sarah knew Abe would be deeply disappointed that she had gone to Salem jail without him, but her father would not get permission to take a second child.

Goody Bishop was brought out of Ingersoll's Ordinary, where she had been kept after her examination. Her hands and feet were shackled. Two sturdy village men boosted her onto the back of a horse.

"I know you, William Smith, and you, Godfrey Lauder! I have served you many times. Is this how you repay my hospitality?" she said harshly.

"Hold your tongue, witch!" the marshal said. "I have a stopper for you if you do not." His stopper was a loop of rough cord, which would be tied around the prisoner's mouth if she proved abusive. Eyeing the gnawed, dirty strands, Goody Bishop complained no more.

Ephraim was given the second position, one horse in front of Marshal Herrick and the prisoner. Sarah would have preferred riding behind Goody Bishop. She could feel the woman's gaze boring into her back as she clung to her father's waist. The one time Sarah dared look back, Goody Bishop had her eyes closed. Her lips were moving silently. If she were anyone else, Sarah would have thought she was praying, but who did a witch pray to but the Devil?

They crossed the wooden bridge over Endicott Creek. The land here was sandy, covered with salt grass, and not good for farming. It was known as Northfields. Houses were few. Soon the road forked. They took the road to Salem Town.

"I know this road," Bridget Bishop announced in a loud voice. "I am a Salem woman, you know." No one answered her. "I tried to buy land here once. Good spot for a tavern, this lonely road betwixt the Farms and Salem Town."

"Quiet," Herrick growled. He was a tough old salt, a sailor come home from the sea. He did not say much, but when he did it had weight.

"Just passing the time," Goody Bishop said pleasantly. She prattled on a bit more until Herrick got out the stopper. He let it dangle from his thumb as he held the reins. Bridget Bishop stopped talking.

They crossed Gardner's Brook and rejoined the west road. There were folk about now, traveling to and from Salem. The sight of an armed party, escorting a matron in chains, drew many curious stares. One young fellow with a pockmarked face trailed after them until Bridget Bishop leaned over and hissed, "Scat!" at him.

It was late afternoon when they arrived. Salem was a pretty town of half-timbered houses and narrow streets, dominated by the masts of anchored ships and seaside warehouses. The lead rider, Constable Braybrook, pointed out the places of interest, including Judge Corwin's home, Judge Hathorne's house, the Salem meetinghouse, and the Ship Tavern. The party turned left after passing the tavern and there was Salem jail. It was a squat, purposeful structure, surrounded on three sides by empty lots. A number of people milled around outside the jail. Sarah saw some were armed with halberds. Others had shackles on their feet.

Marshal Herrick called out, "Whoa-ho!" and the escorts halted. Ephraim got down.

"Stay here for now," he told Sarah.

The jailer, a skeletal man in a long, black coat, came out to accept the new prisoner. Through the open door, Sarah could see the jail was full. People squatted in the main corridor or hung their hands on the barred doors. Other captives lounged outdoors in the bright sunlight. It seemed to Sarah the prisoners could have overcome the small number of guards at any time and run away. They were shackled, but they outnumbered their keepers twenty to one.

Braybrook and Ephraim Wright helped Bridget Bishop down from Herrick's horse. The jailer made his mark on the receipt, took Goody Bishop by the manacles, and led her inside.

"You are discharged," Herrick said to the men hired for the day, including Ephraim. He tipped his high-crowned hat to them and started back to Salem Village.

Sarah studied the prisoners. The terror had spread beyond the village to the neighboring community of Topsfield. Only a few days before, a Topsfield girl, Abigail Hobbs, freely confessed to illicit contact with the Devil. Abe Toothaker eagerly related what he knew of the Hobbs girl. Abigail Hobbs had lived in Falmouth, on Casco Bay. She had openly proclaimed her intimacy with the Devil, claiming she had "sold herself, body and soul, to the Old Boy." She ran free through the countryside in Maine, unafraid of the Wabanaki, for the Devil was her protector. Once identified as a tormentor by the afflicted in Salem Village, Abigail Hobbs was arrested and confessed. Abe heard her say the Devil recruited witches among the settlers dispossessed in the Eastward.

Now at the jail, Sarah wondered if the young blond girl she saw at the jail window was the infamous Abigail Hobbs.

Her father disappeared inside for a time, then returned.

"Do you really want to go in?" he asked. Sarah nodded. "Did you bring the things you wanted to deliver?"

Sarah had collected a number of things she wanted to give to Dorcas Good. She had some tidbits of food—ham, hard-boiled eggs, a tiny wedge of cheese—a small candle stub, a cup-and-ball toy her father whittled out of some soft pine, and a jar of fresh water. These were tied up in an old kerchief Goody Griggs had given her.

"I have them," she said, patting the bundle tied to her apron strings.

"Come, lamb." He held out his hands, catching her under the arms and hoisting her smoothly to the ground.

They went in the front door. Sarah was immediately assaulted by a horrendous odor. The jail floor was dank and wet, and the interior was unlit except by what sunlight filtered through the barred windows. Men and women sat in the corridors on filthy straw, chains around their wrists and ankles. A watchman circulated among them, giving them sips of water from a mossy bucket with a dented tin dipper.

"Why is it so dirty?" she gasped.

"It is thought by many that prisoners do not deserve anything but cruelty and neglect," her father replied.

"That is not Christian!"

"No," Ephraim said. "It is not."

He stopped the water carrier and asked where Dorcas Good was. The warder, as dirty as his charges, spat on the dirt floor.

"Try the back."

Ephraim thanked him and steered Sarah that way. The warder stopped them.

"What's in the cloth? I got to see whatever you bring in here!" he said.

The last thing Sarah wanted was this filthy man rummaging through her gifts. Ephraim, stone-faced, slipped the man a coin and he grinned.

"By your leave," he said, backing aside.

The rear of the jail had two large rooms instead of cells. Several dozen people were crowded into these communal rooms. Ephraim went to the door of the north room and called for Dorcas Good. All he received in reply were coughs and sullen stares.

"Over here."

A woman in the south room beckoned. Ephraim and Sarah crossed the hall.

"She's in with us, poor thing," the woman said. Her clothes were fine, though soiled with jailhouse filth.

"Thank you, goodwife."

Ephraim asked the turnkey to open the door. While this happened the helpful woman said, "I am Mary English. My husband is Philip English, the merchant."

Ephraim paused halfway through the door. "Are you accused of witchcraft, mistress?"

"I am, but I am innocent! I know you are a constable. If you have influence with the judges, could you ask them to let me out? I will not flee—"

"Quiet, witch," growled the turnkey. He smacked his cudgel against the bars. Mary English cried out and drew back.

Ephraim said, "None of these people have been convicted of any crime. I suggest you consider how you treat possibly innocent people!"

The jailer made an obscene remark. Sarah huddled close to her father.

"I shall remember your name, mistress," Ephraim promised Goody English.

The communal room was worse than the hall. The floor was treacherous with muck, and the smell was many times worse. Prisoners sat with their back to the wall—there was no furniture—or stood at the windows, trying to find fresh air. Ephraim asked again, in a low voice, where Dorcas Good might be. He was told to try the back corner.

She was there, seated in a shaft of sunlight slanting in from the window. Her feet were splayed out and her dirty dress spread across her knees. Dorcas was humming and playing with something in the straw.

"Hello, Dorcas," Ephraim said. The little girl did not look up. Sarah questioned her father with a glance. He nodded.

Sarah untied the bundle from her apron and squatted, careful not to touch her knees to the filthy floor.

"I brought you something," she said.

Dorcas' head snapped up. Sarah almost fell backward in surprise. The girl's blue eyes stood out vividly against her dirt-smeared cheeks.

"Do you want to play?" she said.

"What are you playing?" Sarah asked.

"Jacks." She frowned. "But my ball doesn't bounce very well."

Dorcas had made jacks from twisted tufts of straw. Her ball was made of dirt and excrement. She held it out for Sarah. Forcing a faint smile, Sarah opened her bundle and got out the cup-and-ball game Ephraim had made for her.

"Try mine," she said. The ball was tied to the cup with a length of string. Sarah tossed the ball up, caught it in the cup, then tried again. She missed the second time.

"You're not very good," Dorcas said. "Let me!"

She missed three times, then succeeded three times. "See?" she said. "I'm good at games."

"Yes, you are. Why don't you keep it? Here are some other things for you—"

A large hand reached in, brushing Sarah aside.

"You cannot have candles in prison," said a man with a strong voice. "If the straw catches fire, we would perish."

"I am sorry!" Sarah said, wide-eyed.

Ephraim helped her stand. "She was only trying to ease the child's lot," he said.

The man who took the candle stub was gray-haired but strong, and had a proud demeanor. "God bless you for your mercy," he said. "But we must beware of fire here."

He wandered away, carrying the stub. Sarah heard someone say his name was John Proctor.

Dorcas played cup-and-ball with one hand. She paid no attention to the food Sarah had brought. When a woman came up behind Dorcas with designs on taking her gifts, Ephraim blocked her path.

"Out of my way."

It was Dorcas' mother, Sarah Good. Recognizing the reputed witch, Sarah Wright grabbed her father's hand.

"The food is for the girl," Ephraim said.

"I know that. Do you think I would steal from the mouth of my own child?" Sarah Good gathered up the kerchief and its treasures. "Dorcas doesn't know day from night. I will keep this for her, otherwise the vultures in here will steal it."

She was as fierce as ever, but Sarah believed her. "I will pray for you," she said. "And for Dorcas, too."

"Do as you like." Sarah Good tucked the bundle inside her blouse. She took out her pipe, tapped it absently on the heel of her hand, and asked if the Wrights had brought any tobacco. Ephraim said they had not.

"Where is your baby?" Sarah asked. Sarah Good glared at her with narrowed eyes.

"Dead, of fever."

"I am sorry!"

"Bah." She returned to the shadows.

"Come, lamb."

Outside, Sarah could not get the stink of the jail out of her nostrils. She splashed water from the horse trough on her hands and face. It did not help.

As she was washing, two men marched past in heavy shackles. They were Wabanaki, dressed in deerskins. Their paint had been scrubbed off, and judging by their bruises, they had been given a harsh beating. When they passed, the lead Indian stumbled over his chains and sprawled at Sarah's feet. Being so close to one of the tribe who had slain her mother and brother terrified her.

The Wabanaki man got to his hands and knees. He looked at Sarah through blackened, swollen eyes.

"Water," he muttered in English. "Water . . . "

Sarah picked up a dipper. Though speechless with fear, she filled it from the trough. The captive Wabanaki grasped the bowl with battered fingers. He gulped water until the jailer struck him with his cudgel. The dipper fell to the ground. The guards hauled the Indian to his feet.

"My thanks, girl," he said, before being driven inside.

By their hired horse, Sarah said, "Who are those men?"

"Prisoners of war on their way to Boston," her father said.

"What will happen to them?"

"With luck, they will be exchanged for English captives taken by the Indians."

On the horse, Sarah noticed blood on her sleeves. It might have come from one of the accused witches in jail, or else from the captive Wabanaki. Try as she might, she could see no difference between the stains left by English captives or by Indian prisoners of war.

chapter eight

Worse Than Disease

Like ripples from a pebble dropped in a pond, accusations of witchcraft echoed outward from Salem Village in wider and wider circles. By May there were suspects in jail from Andover, Topsfield, Boxford to the north; Wenham, Gloucester, and Beverly to the east; Salem Town and Lynn to the south. The shadow of the Devil's plot came closer to Sarah Wright. In May, "Doctor" Roger Toothaker was arrested. Abe was stunned, but Dr. Griggs expressed a common view when he heard the news.

"It is about time! That quacksalver has been practicing witchcraft for years!"

Sarah found Abe near Ingersoll's Ordinary on May 18. His uncle was due to be questioned by Judge Hathorne and Judge Corwin that morning. Sarah assumed Abe was there to hear the proceedings.

She saw him, red-eyed, skulking outside the shady end of the tavern. She hadn't seen him in over a week. Never tidy, he looked even scruffier than usual. His fingernails were black with grime, and his shirtsleeves were so soiled they looked like they had been dyed brown.

"Abe," Sarah said, "are you well?"

"Oh, aye."

"Are you coming to hear the court?"

He screwed his eyes shut. Tears glistened in the corners.

"Listen, Sarah, there's something you should know," he said, gasping between words. "My uncle, well—" Abe scrubbed a fist against his forehead. "My uncle's not really my uncle, after all." Amazed, Sarah said nothing. Trembling, the boy went on. "He's my father."

"Your father?"

"I only found out after he was taken by the sheriff," Abe said. "My mother told me."

Abe lived in Billerica with his mother and siblings. His mother worked as a washerwoman, but the family survived on the charity of the Billerica town fathers. Abe was her youngest child. To spare him the shame of abandonment, he had been told that Roger Toothaker was his uncle, not his father.

Sarah linked her arm in Abe's. "We don't have to go in."

He shook his head broadly and pulled free. "No. I'll see him answer before the court!"

Compared to the days when Sarah Good or Tituba were questioned, the court was sparsely attended. There had been so many accusations, so many arrests, that many people had begun staying away lest the eyes of the afflicted ones fall on them.

The court had already finished questioning John Willard, accused of murder by witchcraft by Ann Putnam Junior, Mary Warren, and the rest. John Indian was there, screaming that Willard's specter was cutting him with a knife. When the constables held Willard's hands, the phantom torments faded.

In his defense, Willard tried to repeat the Lord's Prayer, a task no sworn witch could do. He tried five times and failed every time. After his last failure, he cried, "It is these wicked ones that do so overcome me!"

He was ordered to jail. Next, the court listened to new arguments about accused witch Mary Esty, a sister of Rebecca Nurse. The afflicted ones were now uncertain about Goody Esty's guilt. Only Mercy Lewis was sure she had been hurt by Esty's specter. Unwilling to hold an old woman of good repute on the word of Mercy Lewis alone, Hathorne and Corwin released Mary Esty to her family.

"Call Roger Toothaker," the bailiff said.

A tall, rawboned man shuffled forward. His hands and feet were chained. In his dusty coat and bareheaded, Sarah thought he looked more like a farmer than a doctor.

"You are Roger Toothaker of Billerica?" Hathorne asked.

"May it please Your Worship, my home is in Salem," he replied. He had a North Country accent, like the Wrights' neighbor in Maine, Goodman Strong.

Ezekiel Cheever, the recorder, made changes in his record. When he was done, Hathorne said, "You are hereby accused of harming Ann Putnam Junior, Abigail Williams, Mary Walcott,

Elizabeth Hubbard, and sundry others with acts of witchcraft. How do you plead?"

Toothaker's eyes darted back and forth. If he recognized Abe, standing a few feet from the open door, he gave no sign.

"I am innocent, Your Worship."

"What evil spirit have you familiarity with?"

"None, sir! I have spent a large part of my life doctoring folks against the Devil."

"You are a medical man?" Hathorne asked coolly.

"I know more about doctoring than most with fancy letters after their names," Toothaker replied.

"You use herbs and roots as medicine?"

Toothaker readily admitted he did.

"Stones? Bark?"

"I use whatever the Good Lord gives me, Your Worship."

Hathorne's brow furrowed. "Do you use urine in your medicaments?"

Toothaker sensed peril. He scuffed his feet back and forth until the judge repeated the question.

"Sometimes, if the sickness calls for it."

Judge Corwin passed Hathorne a piece of paper. Hathorne read it at a glance.

"Does the name Mattheas Button mean anything to you?"

Color drained from Toothaker's face. In a raspy voice, he said, "What's that name again?"

"Mattheas Button, a Billerica man who died eight years ago, of apoplexy. You knew him, did you not?"

"No, Your Worship. I never met him."

Hathorne held up the paper Corwin had given him. "I have here the deposition of William Keene, of Billerica. In it he states you made a charm consisting of a tightly stoppered bottle, some iron nails, and the urine of an afflicted child. This bottle you placed in the fireplace of said Keene until the vessel burst from the heat. What happened then to Mattheas Button?"

White as chalk, Roger Toothaker did not answer. To Sarah's horror, Abe spoke out.

"The witch died! When the bottle busted, the witch died!"

"Be silent in court!" Hathorne said sternly. Sarah tugged Abe back against the wall.

"You are now before authority!" Hathorne boomed. "Did you make a charm that resulted in a man's death?"

"It was the judgment of God," Toothaker said.

"Judgment of God? Which God?" Roger Toothaker did not answer. "Having thus slain a likely servant of the Devil, you have since become a witch yourself, have you not?"

"Not so, Your Worship—"

"Your shape appears to the afflicted ones. We have the testimony of Abigail Williams, Elizabeth Hubbard, Mercy Lewis, and Goodwife Sarah Bibber that your shape did grievously bite, pinch, and stab them until blood flowed. Do you deny it?"

"It—it cannot be true, sir. I am an honest Christian."

Betty Hubbard lunged from the pack of girls, foam spewing from her lips. "He burns me!" she shrieked. "He burns me with a brand of fire! He burns me!"

Toothaker spread his manacled hands in a gesture of harmlessness. Sarah Bibber cried out as if she were struck in the eyes by the spectral hands of Roger Toothaker.

"The evidence of your guilt is plain." With a withering glare, Hathorne signed papers committing the self-made doctor to jail.

Toothaker was taken out between a pair of constables. They marched past Sarah and Abe. For a fleeting moment, the wayward doctor and his youngest son's eyes met. Then the officers thrust Roger Toothaker out the door.

Sarah waited a decent interval, then led Abe outside. The wagonload of prisoners for Boston jail was almost out of sight.

"Come along, Abe." Sarah guided Abe away. Behind them, the meetinghouse rang with frightful screams.

Near the turnoff for Dr. Griggs' house, Sarah said, "I'm sure he will be freed, Abe. A doctor would not be a witch—"

"Why not?" Abe snapped. They were his first words since leaving the court. "He knows about charms and magic, and the afflicted ones see his shape!"

"Maybe they are wrong," Sarah said. "Maybe the Devil can assume any shape he wishes."

"He is a wicked man," Abe said bitterly. "He left us to starve! Who else but a witch would let his children go hungry?"

He pulled free of Sarah's grasp and ran. Abe shouted, "I hope he hangs!"

Sarah watched him go, running as hard as he could up the north road.

chapter nine

Demon Shapes

The next blow against Satan was a mighty one. Reverend George Burroughs was arrested for practicing evil magic.

Sarah remembered him from Maine. He was the short, overbearing man who had tried to talk her father into joining the militia after their farm was destroyed. He had been appearing in the visions of the afflicted ones for some time, and he was brought to the Bay Colony for examination. Reverend Burroughs fared badly. In addition to the fits and torments of the accusers, people who had known him in the Eastward testified about unnatural acts Burroughs had committed. He was strangely strong for such a small man. It was said he could raise a long-barreled gun by sticking his finger in the muzzle and holding it out at arm's length. Others testified that they had seen Reverend Burroughs lift a barrel of molasses out of a canoe and carry it ashore, simply by hooking two fingers on the bung.

Oddly, for a minister, he had not baptized his younger children. This was thought to be proof of his sworn allegiance to the Devil. The afflicted girls added murder to the charges when they claimed to have seen the ghosts of Reverend Burroughs' deceased wives, who claimed their husband murdered them. The judges consigned Burroughs to jail to await trial.

The circle of accused witches had grown enormously beyond Tituba's original confession. At first the accused were poor and powerless women like Sarah Good and Goody Osburn. Next, suspicion fell on villagers with shady or quarrelsome reputations. Martha Cory fell into this group, as did her husband, Giles, the Proctors, and Bridget Bishop. Later, the accusations included people of good reputation but minor means, like Rebecca Nurse and her sisters, Sarah Cloyse and Mary Esty.

By the end of May 1692, people of substance were under suspicion: merchant Philip English, his wife, Reverend Burroughs, Captain Nathaniel Cary, and his wife. Sarah could not imagine why wealthy, notable people would be witches. How could the Devil tempt those who had everything?

"What can it mean that prominent people are called witches?" Sarah wondered.

"It means deception," her father said.

"The Devil deceives the afflicted ones?"

"I cannot speak for them, but I see certain people accused who are alien or unliked, despite their wealth or place." Reverend Burroughs had once served as minister in Salem Village and was widely unpopular there. Philip English was wealthy—a target of envy—and his real name was Anglais, the French version of "English."

Demon Shapes

A new governor, Sir William Phips, a man of great energy, had taken office on May 16. Faced with jails bulging with accused witches, he authorized a special Court of Oyer and Terminer (meaning "to hear and to determine") to try witchcraft cases. His lieutenant governor, William Stoughton, would be chief justice. Also on the court would be John Hathorne, Jonathan Corwin, Samuel Sewall, Bartholomew Gedney, John Richards, Nathaniel Saltonstall, Wait Still Winthrop, and Peter Sergeant. These were the most illustrious men in the colony. If anyone could sort out the workings of the Devil, surely these learned men could.

Ephraim was not so certain. He had grown increasingly somber since their trip to Salem jail. Hard money was scarce. The war in the Eastward dragged on. Taxes were heavy, but many colonial salaries went unpaid. There was no money to pay them. Ephraim's last constabulary job, escorting Reverend Burroughs to Boston jail, was paid in coin, but Sheriff Corwin told him henceforth he would be paid in scrip. Scrip was just a paper promise by the colony to pay the holder in the future. Scrip was difficult to spend. Merchants seldom took it at face value. Farmers refused it altogether.

While Ephraim brooded, Sarah walked or rode around the county on errands for her hosts. She learned where everyone lived in Salem Village and met most of them. The one person she did not see was Abe Toothaker. Abe had not been seen in the village since his father's hearing. He was gone so long Sarah sought out his mother, Mary Toothaker.

"I have heard much about you from Absalom," she said, standing at the door of her tumbledown cottage. "I am glad to know he has such a kind friend."

Sarah asked where Abe was. Goody Toothaker frowned. "He's run off to Salem Town."

"But why?"

"To be near his worthless father, I expect. He will return when he gets hungry enough."

With that, Mary Toothaker shut the door, so Sarah went on her way.

The Court of Oyer and Terminer convened on June 2, at the courthouse in Salem Town. The witch trials had outgrown Salem Village. Sarah's father was called as a witness against Bridget Bishop. Ephraim dusted off his coat and hat, borrowed a horse from Farmer Flint, and set out for Salem Town early Thursday morning. Sarah rode behind him.

A stream of people filled the roads south to Salem Town, bound for the trials. Sarah saw single men on horseback, families in carts, men leading their wives on donkeys, and folks of every sort walking. It was a considerable journey on foot. People walking would be lucky to hear any of the proceedings before the noon recess.

Salem's courthouse was a two-story brick building, substantial but plain. Trials were held on the second floor. The ground floor was used by a Latin grammar school. As a witness, Ephraim was ushered through the press of people crowding the door.

Sarah and Ephraim sat close-packed on a bench behind the advocates' rail. At the front of the room sat the justices: Mr. Stoughton, presiding chief justice, along with Mr. Sewall, Mr. Gedney, Mr. Richards, and Mr. Saltonstall. Judge Hathorne, who questioned the accused witches so vigorously in Salem Village, was also present.

At eight o'clock, Chief Justice Stoughton called the court to order. The first witnesses gave testimony about accused witches Rebecca Nurse, Elizabeth Howe, Elizabeth Proctor, John Willard, Sarah Good, Bridget Bishop, and Alice Parker. There was disturbing testimony about searches done of the accused witches' bodies. The court wanted to know if any unnatural "marks or teats" were found on any of them. Witches were said to nurse demons with their own blood, and where the familiars sucked there was supposed to be a telltale mark.

Goody Bishop, Goody Nurse, and Goody Proctor all had "excrescences of flesh" in private parts of their bodies. These were declared unnatural, though Rebecca Nurse claimed that hers were a result of childbirth.

Once these findings were given, the trial of Bridget Bishop began. Goody Bishop was brought forward in chains.

The indictment was read to her, and the bailiff asked the required question, "How do you plead?"

"Not guilty!" Goody Bishop declared.

"How will you be tried?"

"By God and my country!"

Her entire history was presented. Her first husband, Goodman Wasslebee, died back in England. Shapes of the dead appearing to the afflicted in Salem Village claimed he was murdered. No evidence was offered other than these spectral whisperings.

Bridget Wasslebee emigrated to Salem Town and married Thomas Oliver. Bridget and Thomas were not a happy couple. They fought, often coming to blows, and Bridget was seen about town with black eyes and swollen lips. She gave as good as she got, though, and Thomas Oliver bore the marks of her rage as well. In 1677, they were tried for disturbing the peace, found guilty, and given the choice of paying a fine or standing in the market square with a sign describing their crime. Thomas Oliver's daughter by a previous marriage paid his fine, but Bridget Bishop had to stand in shame.

In 1670, Goody Oliver was accused of witchcraft for the first time. She was charged with bewitching a slave belonging to Nathaniel Ingersoll's brother, John. The court released her then, citing a lack of evidence. By 1687, Thomas Oliver was dead and Bridget was married to Edward Bishop.

There was the sad story of Samuel Shattuck's child, who lost his reason after Goody Bishop scratched his forehead. Ephraim explained to Sarah that drawing blood from a witch's face was believed to be a countercharm to her magic. If the witch drew blood from her victim instead, the poor sufferer was doomed.

Most damaging was the testimony about some small cloth puppets, pierced through with long pins, found in what had once been Goody Bishop's house. This was plain evidence of spell casting.

When asked by Judge Stoughton about the witch dolls in her old house, Goody Bishop said, "If I had made such things, would I send men there to discover them?"

"Criminals are not perfect reasoners," Stoughton replied. "You may have forgotten your long-ago deed."

Sarah found Judge Stoughton as forbidding as any witch. He was white-haired and gray-faced, with a long, thin nose and a mouth so small she thought it could be covered by a single button. There was no warmth in his eyes, and still less in his voice.

Ephraim was called at last. He gave his oath and faced the judges.

"Goodman Wright, you were lately engaged as a constable by the sheriff of Essex County?" asked the King's attorney general, Thomas Newton.

"I was, Your Worship."

"Did you participate in the arrest of said Bishop?"

"No, sir. I was not present when Goody Bishop was arrested. I was when she was taken to jail in Salem Town."

Newton said, "Can you describe what happened when Bishop was being brought to jail?"

"Yes, Your Worship." Ephraim glanced at the judges, then at the prisoner, facing him a few feet away. Though shackled, Goody Bishop's stance was defiant.

"When we passed the Salem meetinghouse, she stared hard at the building. There was a noise from within after she did so."

"And what was the cause of the noise?" Newton asked.

"Part of a partition had come down."

"Fell, you mean?"

"No, sir, it was halfway across the meeting room from where it had been nailed," Ephraim answered, somewhat reluctantly.

"A partition, nailed to two posts, tore loose and flew across the room of the empty meetinghouse, simply because the prisoner Bishop cast her eye on the building?" Without waiting for Ephraim to agree or not, Newton added, "Thank you, goodman. You are dismissed."

Ephraim sat down again. Sarah could tell he was unhappy, but she was not sure why.

The jury did not take long to decide Goody Bishop's fate. They unanimously agreed Bridget Bishop was guilty on all counts. Chief Justice Stoughton ordered the prisoner to face the bench.

"It is the judgment of this court that you be guilty of the crime of witchcraft. Do you have anything to say for yourself?"

"I am innocent!" Goody Bishop declared. "If I were guilty, you would know it!"

Many in the audience gasped. The prisoner had just threatened the chief justice! Stoughton regarded Goody Bishop coldly.

"Bridget Bishop, alias Oliver, in the name of God, and Their Majesties King William and Queen Mary, I hereby sentence you to death. On a date to be chosen by the court you shall be conveyed to a place of execution and there be hanged by the neck until you are dead. May God have mercy on your soul!"

"Mercy? What mercy is there in this madhouse?" Bridget Bishop cried. Two marshals seized her arms. She struggled. "My blood is on your hands!"

"Take her away," said Stoughton as coolly as he might order meat at a tavern. He announced a short recess for lunch. More defendants were to be tried in the afternoon, but since Ephraim was excused as a witness, he took Sarah away.

Bridget Bishop was ordered to hang just eight days later, on June 10, 1692.

The night before Goody Bishop was hanged, the village byways were vacant, the fields empty. Sarah kept close to the Griggses' hearth. For her faithful work all spring, Goody Griggs had given Sarah her own psalm book. It was the first book of any sort she had ever owned. That evening she sat by the fire, reading Psalm 86. She had just reached the fifth verse: "'For thou, Lord, art good and ready to forgive; and plenteous in mercy unto all of them that call upon thee—'"

There was a modest knock on the door.

Dr. Griggs put aside his pipe and went to see who it was. Ephraim stood up, out of the line of sight of the open door.

"Why, it's the Toothaker boy. What brings you here at this hour?"

"May I see Miss Sarah, please, sir?"

Her father nodded his permission. She went to the door. Dr. Griggs returned to his chair and pipe.

"Can you come out?" asked Abe in a low voice.

"Yes, but not for long." She took a shawl from a peg by the door. After the heat of the fire, the twilight air felt chilly.

"I come from Salem Town," he said. "They are hanging the witch tomorrow. I am going to see. Will you come with me?"

"I do not want to see anyone hanged."

"She's a witch. She's hurt good Christian folk and sold her soul to the Devil. She ought to hang. That's the law."

Sarah did not understand Abe. His own father, wayward though he may have been, was facing charges of witchcraft. Had he no sympathy for the accused?

"I can't go by myself," Abe said. "Reverend Noyes said it would be very instruck—instructive, but someone has to go with me so it is a lesson and not a lark." Nicholas Noyes was the minister of the Salem meeting.

She looked at the fence rails, black against the sky. Abe pleaded, "Please, Sarah. As I am your friend, go with me tomorrow."

With his scarecrow clothes and hollow cheeks, Abe was in sad shape. Much as she hated the idea, she agreed.

He gripped her hand. "Good! Go to the meadow on the west side of the Salem Town bridge. That's where they'll do it!"

Sarah said good-bye. He lingered a moment as though wanting to say something more. When she reached the door, he mumbled a farewell.

"That boy ought not be allowed to roam the countryside," Goody Griggs intoned once Sarah had returned.

"There's no one to look after him," the doctor said. "Have you not heard? Goody Toothaker has been arrested."

Sarah was dumbstruck. If Abe's mother was under arrest for witchcraft, Abe had no one at all. Was that what he was trying to tell her before he left?

Sarah threw wide the door and ran out into the yard. "Abe!" she called. "Abe, where are you?"

Spring clouds had thickened overhead, blotting out the moon and stars. Ten yards from the Griggs house, there was nothing but darkness.

Sarah struggled all night with her promise to Abe. What would her father think if he discovered she was going to see the hanging? Far into the night she begged God for an answer to her problem. Eventually, it came. Goody Bishop was going to die, whether Sarah was there or not. If witnessing the death of Bridget Bishop could make Abe feel pity for the accused, then it might help reconcile him to his father.

Weary from her unhappy night, she rose before dawn and dressed. She thought her father was still asleep, but when she descended from the loft she found him standing by the hearth, poking the embers to raise a flame.

"Lamb? You are up early."

"I promised to meet Abe this morning," she said. "If that pleases you, Father."

Under his prodding a charred length of wood broke in two and started to crackle. Ephraim said, "You are a true friend to that boy."

"When we came to the village, he was the first person to befriend me. People despise him because he is poor, but he is good and true."

Ephraim put down the poker. "I will tell Goody Griggs you have gone out. Will you be back by afternoon?" She vowed she would be. "Go with God, then, daughter."

Sarah slipped outside, shivering. The morning sky was clear, the air promising to be hot. Tying her cap strings, she hurried on her way.

It was a long walk. She saw many people on their way to the execution.

The spot chosen was a hill in a meadow not far from the town bridge. There was a lone maple tree near the summit, surrounded by high spring grass. When Sarah reached the meadow, there were several hundred people already there. The Salem Town Militia had formed a line leading from the road to the tree. People were kept back by lines of crossed pikes.

It took her a while to find Abe. He came bounding through the grass, waving wildly. In deference to the solemn occasion, he did not shout.

They met at the foot of the hill. Sarah and Abe clasped hands.

"You are here!" he said.

"I am here," Sarah said firmly. Their greeting was cut short by the rattle of a drum.

Down the road from Salem Town came a procession. Leading it was a drummer boy, followed by six mounted constables in polished steel helmets. Behind them came a two-wheel cart drawn by a bullock. Standing in the back, her red paragon bodice still bright enough to catch the eye, was Bridget Bishop.

Next came Sheriff George Corwin and a quartet of deputies. A minister in black robes followed on foot, reading aloud from his Bible as he strode along. People in the crowd identified him as John Hale of Beverly. Trailing the black-garbed Hale was a crowd of people from Salem Town. They were all sorts: young, old, men, women, and children. Hangings were rare in Salem, and a witch execution was even rarer.

The drummer reached the tree and halted. He continued his tattoo until the cart arrived. Two constables stood by the open end of the cart and waited for Goody Bishop to alight. She did not move, so the men climbed in and dragged her out.

"Let me go! I am innocent! I am not a witch!" she protested loudly.

"Be silent, or be gagged!" Sheriff Corwin retorted.

On the ground, Bridget Bishop's manacles were removed. Her hands were drawn behind her back and lashed together with heavy cord.

"You cannot do this!" she said, appealing to the crowd. "You are killing an innocent woman!"

"Bridget Bishop! You have been found guilty of the foul crime of witchcraft by a jury of your countrymen. It is the judgment of the Court of Oyer and Terminer, of the Colony of Massachusetts, that you be hanged by neck until you are dead," the sheriff recited.

"Fools! Dupes! You've been deceived!" she cried as the hangman approached. He was a rough-looking fellow in a leather vest, with a tattered, wide-brimmed hat on his head.

"Do your duty," Corwin said. The hangman took a black cloth bag from inside his vest. When he pulled this over Bridget Bishop's head, she stopped struggling.

"Thank you for the cowl," she said bitterly. "I saw a hanged man's face once. It was not a sight for decent folk to see."

With the hood in place, the hangman took Goody Bishop by the arm. He marched her to the foot of the tree. With the other hand, he flung the noose high over a stout limb, making a perfect throw on the first try.

Two men ran forward with a ladder. It was uncommonly wide, Sarah saw, big enough for two to climb abreast. The men leaned it against the tree and withdrew. The hangman tested its steadiness by kicking the lowest rung a few times. He signaled the constables to bring the prisoner.

They half dragged Bridget Bishop to the ladder, supporting her until she gained the first rung. Two steps above, the hangman stooped to take her by the arm. She said something to him. It was muffled by the hood. He replied in a low voice.

When she was well more than her height off the ground, the hangman stopped Goody Bishop. He caught the dangling noose and worked the loop over her head.

Sarah turned away and shut her eyes. She could hear the minister, Mr. Hale, reciting the Lord's Prayer.

"—*innocent!*" Bridget Bishop managed to shout through the cloth.

Mr. Hale concluded, "'For Thine is the Kingdom, and the Power, and the Glory, forever. Amen.'"

Sarah heard a creak, a thud, and the crowd went "Oh!" A great lump formed in her throat. She tried several times to swallow it, without success.

A hand touched her shoulder. Sarah opened her eyes. Everyone present gazed at the same thing: the slowly swinging body of Bridget Bishop. Only Sarah was looking away—Sarah, and the kindly looking man beside her.

"Do not avert your eyes," Reverend Hale said gently. "Behold God's judgment."

She shook her head and squeezed her eyes shut again. Hale knelt in front of her.

"This is a terrible consummation of a misspent soul," he said calmly. "Do not throw away the only good that will come of Bridget Bishop's life."

Sarah looked at him, puzzled. "What good?" she asked, voice choked.

"The lesson of the wages of sin," Mr. Hale said. Sarah remembered her father's wry use of those words when he exposed Bridget Bishop's crooked shovel-board.

Reverend Hale slowly turned her around.

Like some horrible pendulum, the lifeless body of Bridget Bishop swung back and forth. The crowd had been quiet at the moment of execution. Now talk began again, growing louder with each swing of the corpse. What Sarah heard most was speculation about who would be hanged next. The name most often mentioned was Sarah Good.

She cast about for Abe. He was a few steps away, on both knees in the trampled grass. His hands were clasped under his chin. Sarah thought he might be praying, but his eyes were open and tears coursed down his dirty cheeks.

He went back to Salem Town without saying a word. Sarah did not even have a chance to ask him where he was staying. Alone, she walked all the way back to Dr. Griggs' house.

When she reached home there were men and horses in the doctor's yard. She recognized Reverend Parris, Thomas Putnam, and several of his kinsmen. Her father stood in the midst of them. No one was shouting, but the words reaching Sarah sounded heated.

"All I want is what I am owed," Ephraim was saying, "nothing more."

"Neither the village nor the county has coin, for you or anyone else," Thomas Putnam said. "There is scrip—"

"Useless paper," Ephraim scoffed.

"What about payment in kind?" asked Reverend Parris.

"What kind?"

The elder Putnam and the minister of Salem Village exchanged glances.

"Cattle?" Putnam said.

Ephraim said, "I have no place to quarter cows."

"Land?" Reverend Parris said.

"What land does the village own?" Ephraim asked.

"None just now, but we should be able to acquire property owned by the witches. They have debts to the colony that must be paid. We could set aside a parcel for you."

Anger welled in her father's face. Sarah thought he would strike Reverend Parris, but he mastered his ire and said, "I want hard money, thank you. My service is ended until I am paid!"

Thomas Putnam looked grim. "It is said you pay visits to jailed witches, bringing them comforts. You have refused to arrest others accused. Are you so mercenary, Goodman Wright, or merely a friend of witches?"

"You are done here!" Ephraim declared. "I am sure you have pressing business elsewhere!"

Stone-faced, Reverend Parris and his supporters got on their horses and left. They galloped away so vigorously that Sarah had to duck and weave to avoid their horses.

Ephraim took her in his arms. "Mind the child!" he shouted at the men's backs.

"Father, what has happened?"

"They wanted me to serve as a constable again. I told them I would not serve unless I was paid in hard money."

Sarah knew this was an excuse. Ephraim had long been troubled by the widening circle of accusations and arrests. It was possible to believe characters like Bridget Bishop or Sarah Good were in league with the Devil, but what about the gentle Goodwife Nurse and her sisters? Old farmers like John Proctor or Giles Cory?

"My work for Dr. Griggs is done," Ephraim said. "It's time we found our own place."

They walked to the house. Ephraim said, "You went there today, did you not?"

Gazing at the ground, she admitted she had.

"I have been in eight battles and five sieges, and none of them were as awful as a hanging. I am sorry you have seen it."

Sarah was sorry, too. She wondered how anyone, from Reverend Hale to Absalom Toothaker, could believe any good could come from the death of Bridget Bishop.

chapter ten

Taken

A few days after Bridget Bishop's execution, Roger Toothaker died in prison. Like Sarah Osburn and Sarah Good's baby, he died of a fever contracted in jail. Because prisoners were charged a daily fee for their own confinement—as if they were staying in an inn, rather than prison—he owed money to the colonial government. Roger Toothaker's family could not afford to pay his bill. The City of Boston buried the self-made doctor in a pauper's grave without ceremony or a marker.

When Sarah heard about Abe's father's death, she tried to find her friend. He was somewhere in Salem Town, but she could not get there on her own. She wrote a letter to Reverend Noyes on the chance he might see Abe at meeting. But the reverend replied in a short note denying he even knew Abe.

By midsummer, Sarah and her father were ready to leave Dr. Griggs. Ephraim had saved up a small sum from his work on the house and as a constable. They rented a tract of land south of the village, near Dodge's Grist Mill. The plot bordered an inlet called Bass River. It was a good, sunny spot in summer, well suited to growing corn. In winter, Ephraim was warned, it was terribly cold and windy.

There was a small wattle-and-daub house on the hillside with a mossy, shingled roof. Inside was a single room, divided in the middle by the fireplace. They moved in, and Ephraim began searching for seed corn and a plow to hire. There was just enough time left in the season to grow a single crop of corn.

Planting kept the Wrights busy, but it did not change events unfolding around them. The plague of witchcraft was not stifled by the death of Bridget Bishop. In mid-June, Sarah Good went on trial for her life. Her baby had died in prison. Dorcas Good, removed to the Boston jail, had become so distracted she hardly knew her name. With no one to live for and no one on her side, Sarah Good went to trial. There was no shortage of witnesses against her. She was quickly convicted and sentenced to hang.

The same fate befell Rebecca Nurse. Despite every effort of her friends and children, the afflicted ones swore her life away. She was found guilty and scheduled to die with Sarah Good, as were three others: Elizabeth Howe, Susannah Martin, and Sarah Wildes. On July 19, the women were taken from Salem jail to the same lonely hill where Bridget Bishop died. When she reached the gallows, Sarah Good spoke her last in a fashion true to herself.

Reverend Nicholas Noyes of Salem Town was widely known as a jolly man. He detested witchcraft, though; facing the condemned women, he called upon them to confess their guilt so that God might forgive them. Rebecca Nurse spoke eloquently,

leaving some witnesses convinced of her innocence. Crafty Susannah Martin, who had been thought a witch for years, was not about to admit anything. Elizabeth Howe and Sarah Wildes were too frightened to speak, but Sarah Good did.

"I'll not confess the first thing!" she said.

"Come now, you are a witch, and you know you are a witch!" Noyes said. His round face shone with sweat in the hot July sun.

"You are a liar. I am no more a witch than you are a wizard, and if you take my life away, God will give you blood to drink!"

Sarah Wright heard this from Goody Griggs, who was there. When Sarah Good pronounced her curse on Reverend Noyes, the restless crowd fell still. Mr. Noyes grew so pale that many thought he would expire on the spot.

He did not, and the trials went on. Six witches were dead, and the terror continued. Spirits and devils prowled the countryside by day and night, tormenting whomever they could. The hunt for witches went on.

After Sarah Good, the most famous pending case was that of Reverend George Burroughs. The judges were severe with him—the treason of a minister who turned to the Devil was hard for them to stomach—and Burroughs did badly at his trial. When questioned, his answers were evasive, and when he tried to read a prepared statement to the court arguing that witchcraft was impossible, his source was recognized. Burroughs had copied his argument from a book. Plagiarism did not help his case.

Burroughs was convicted and sentenced to death. Sarah was amazed. She knew Reverend Burroughs was a braggart and a bully, but a servant of the Devil? How could that be?

Convicted with him were Martha Carrier (Abe Toothaker's aunt and a bad-tempered woman), John Willard, George Jacobs Senior, and John Proctor, all farmers of formerly decent reputation. The day set for their execution was August 19.

The day arrived hot and still. Ephraim and Sarah were at work in the cornfield early, before the heat became intolerable. Ephraim hauled water in buckets to the field. Sarah chopped weeds with a hoe. The sky was dotted with towering clouds, bright white at the top and gray at the bottom, pregnant with rain.

At midmorning, riders appeared atop the hill. Four hovered on the height, looking down on the Wrights' small farm. They remained there until four more mounted men joined them, then they descended together.

Sarah shaded her eyes. Ephraim poured the last drops from his bucket onto the thirsty soil.

"Is that the sheriff?" she asked.

Ephraim gave the approaching riders a cursory glance. "I do not see him." He picked up the other bucket. Though he had already emptied it, he mimed pouring it on the cornrow.

"What are you doing?" Sarah asked, puzzled.

"Sometimes it is best to pretend you are not concerned."

The riders fanned out in a wide semicircle around Ephraim and Sarah. She knew several of the men from her father's work as a law officer.

"How goes the planting?" Marshal Herrick asked.

"We are late, and the earth thirsts for rain," Ephraim replied. "God willing, we will make up the difference."

"I am sorry, Goodman Wright," Herrick said. "We are here to arrest you."

Sarah opened her mouth to protest. Ephraim hushed her. Sarah saw him reverse his grip on the bucket handle. There was something both furtive and aggressive about his movement.

"On what charge?"

"You are complained of," Constable Braybrook said. He meant that bewitched persons were saying the spirit of Ephraim Wright was hurting them.

"Who complains of me?" he demanded.

Herrick read the warrant, "Samuel Parris, Thomas Putnam, and others on behalf of Abigail Williams, Elizabeth Hubbard, Mercy Lewis, and others. Goodwife Sarah Bibber complains of you for herself."

"That is rot, and you know it!"

"Nevertheless, the complaint is made. You must come with us," Herrick said.

Ephraim hefted the stout wooden bucket. "I am no witch!"

Two of the constables—Salem Town men, unknown to Sarah—leveled carbines at Ephraim. Sarah's heart hammered.

"Come peacefully, Goodman Wright. You may crack my head with your bucket, but the others here will shoot you down like a dog."

Face hard, Ephraim slowly handed the bucket to Sarah. The carbine muzzles followed his every movement. Braybrook dismounted and tied Ephraim's hands with cord.

"Where are you taking me?"

"Salem jail."

"What about my daughter?"

Herrick said, "I have no orders regarding her."

The constables boosted Ephraim onto a horse behind Braybrook. Sarah ran up, clutching her father's leg.

"Father, what shall I do?"

"Go to Dr. Griggs. He will look after you."

Braybrook told her to stand clear. The men rode slowly away. Sarah followed. She could not believe her father was being arrested on suspicion of witchcraft. A more Christian man did not live in Massachusetts. It must be a mistake—a horrible, ghastly error.

She followed them until she saw Dodge's Mill turning slowly close by. Sarah ran to the mill and pounded on the door. Goodman Dodge came to the door. Sarah pointed to the officers departing with her father.

"They are taking him away!" she cried. "Can you help me?"

Goodman Dodge was an old man, crusty and independent. An old soldier, he and Ephraim had discovered they were much alike.

"I got a jenny," he said, squinting at the dwindling horsemen.

Sarah threw a blanket on Dodge's mule, Kate. With a rope halter as her only guide, she urged the old jenny out of her pen.

"I'll bring her back!" she called to the mill owner.

"See that you do! I value that beast more than most people 'round here!"

The officers followed the mill stream, then bore north past Leach's Hill. Sarah kept them in sight, but stopped at the Griggs house to rouse the doctor and his wife. They were not home. Sarah remembered what day it was. The Griggses must have gone to see the hangings.

The road south to Salem Town was thick with people going to Gallows Hill. They slowed Sarah, but they held up the constables, too. Sarah was able to keep them in sight.

Kate panted in the heat. So did Sarah. A lady in a farm cart gave her a drink of spring water. She pushed on. By the time she reached Stone's Plain, the roads were impassable due to the crowds. Sarah struck out across country. When she reached Gallows Hill, the great mob had solidified. She could get no farther. Some distance ahead, Sarah could see her father sitting behind Constable Braybrook.

The condemned witches were already at the tree. George Burroughs was speaking. Sarah was too far away to hear him, but the import of his words echoed through the crowd. Reverend Burroughs was repeating the Lord's Prayer.

It was common knowledge that witches were incapable of saying the Lord's Prayer without error. Reverend Burroughs evidently said it perfectly. Many in the crowd began to mutter. Perhaps Burroughs was innocent. How could a witch pronounce the Lord's own prayer so well?

"See! See!" a voice shouted nearby. Sarah turned and saw both Ann Putnams, Junior and Senior, riding in a wagon with some kinsmen from Salem Village. The younger Ann was shouting. "See how the Devil stands by the little minister? He prompts his every word!"

Many were swayed by her vision of the unseen. The execution went on. The prisoners were kicked off the ladder into sudden death. A collective groan went through the large crowd. Ann Putnam Junior sat down. Her mother held her close as they stared at the hanging figures.

"Good people, hearken to my words!"

A man in black clothes, wearing the white stock of an ordained minister, rode slowly through the crowd on a fine horse. "Good people, do not be swayed by what you heard! 'Tis often said a witch cannot speak the name of God, or the words of our Lord's Prayer, but this is not always so. The Devil spreads such stories to undermine our faith in God. Does the Bible not tell us the Devil can be transformed into an angel of light by his wicked machinations?"

The learned gentleman spoke so earnestly that the crowd forgot its suspicions. Sarah wondered who the minister was, then she heard someone call him Reverend Mather. There were two famous Mathers in Massachusetts, father and son. The man on the black horse was younger than Ephraim, so he must be the son, Cotton Mather.

Bit by bit the crowd dissolved. Ephraim and the constables pushed on. Sarah followed.

Taken

Passing the maple tree, Sarah kept her eyes on the ground. She prayed silently for the souls of the departed, damned by witchcraft or not. The mule trod stolidly ahead.

Don't look, don't look, Sarah thought. The creak of ropes was bad enough, then Sarah spotted a shoe in the grass. It was a man's shoe, smaller than most, and well-worn. There was a hole in the bottom, patched with a scrap of paper. It had come off George Burroughs when he dropped. That empty shoe would haunt Sarah for the rest of her days.

chapter eleven

Signs and Portents

Salem Town was unnaturally idle when Sarah arrived. Governor Phips, afraid French warships would seize colonial ships, had temporarily halted trade and fishing. Nets hung drying in the sun, and the wharves were empty.

Sarah rode through the quiet streets. When she reached the jail, the deputy constables were departing. The jail was more crowded than ever, even though many prisoners had been transferred to Boston. Ignoring the sullen stares and pleas of other accused witches, Sarah went to the door and asked for the jailer. He was not to be found. It was fearfully hot inside the jail, and the stench was overwhelming. Guards roved here and there, hitting unruly prisoners with clubs. A young woman clutched the barred window, weeping uncontrollably. Unable to find her father, Sarah retreated to the street.

Not knowing what to do, she sat on the curb, holding Kate's halter. Time passed. The sun sank behind her, throwing the jail and the street into shadow. Worn out from the day's events,

Sarah nodded where she sat. Sometime later the mule leaned over and nudged her awake. Sarah patted Kate's muzzle and opened her eyes. She was not alone. A boy sat beside her.

"Oh!" She flinched, then realized her company was Abe Toothaker. She barely recognized him. He was clean. His hair was cut and combed, and he wore a tidy, though patched, suit of clothes.

"Mercy!" she said. "Is that you, Abe?"

Sheepishly, he admitted it was. "Why are you here?" he asked. Sarah's eyes burned. She covered them with her sleeve. Sarah explained that her father had been arrested on charges of witchcraft.

"I knew it would happen," Abe said sadly. "I heard Goody Putnam and Goody Bibber say they were beaten with a sword by the specter of your father."

"What nonsense!" The charge was ridiculous. Her father, beating women with a sword?

Sizing up Abe, Sarah said, "How came you to this elegant state?"

"Reverend Higginson took me in."

Reverend John Higginson was the elder minister of Salem. He had retired, leaving his flock to the care of Reverend Noyes. Abe had been wandering the streets of Salem after his mother was arrested, eating out of rubbish bins, even stealing food to keep alive. Reverend Higginson found him and took him in.

"I am sorry about your father," Sarah said. "And your mother."

"My mother's no witch!" Abe said. "How could they accuse her? No better Christian woman ever lived!" He stared at the jail. "This isn't right. Your father's a good man. My mother's no witch, either. How could this happen?"

Sarah tried hard not to cry, but her fears, collected for so long, welled out in a torrent. Abe laid his arm across her shoulders.

"Don't weep, Sarah. Good people like my mother and your father will be well, I'm sure. God will not allow them to suffer."

She raised her tear-stained face to his. "They hanged Rebecca Nurse, as good a woman as ever lived in Massachusetts! They hanged a minister today, Mr. Burroughs! Your father died in that filthy dungeon—why do you think your mother or my father will fare any better?"

Shaken, Abe had no answer. As the shadows lengthened around them, he said, "Come away with me to Reverend Higginson's."

Abe took Sarah by the hand and led the mule. Little more than a block away, they came to Reverend Higginson's house. Abe tied the mule to a tree and knocked on the front door.

An elderly man, white-haired and gaunt, answered the door. He was tall and unbowed, with an alabaster face set off by his somber garb.

"Absalom, there you are! Where have you been, you ragamuffin?"

Abe pulled Sarah forward. Reverend Higginson's eyesight was evidently poor. He did not notice the girl until she was directly in front of his nose.

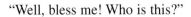

"Well, bless me! Who is this?"

"Sarah Wright, if you please, sir." She curtsied.

"Bless me! What a well-spoken child! What brings you to my door?"

"She's got trouble," Abe said in a low voice.

"*Has* trouble," Reverend Higginson corrected. "What is the problem, child?"

"My father has been taken as a witch!" she blurted.

Reverend Higginson's kindly smile evaporated. "You had best come in," he said.

Sarah and Abe slipped inside. Higginson's house was small but well-made. In the front room, a candle burned. A table was there, littered with sheets of foolscap covered with writing. An inkwell stood open. Two newly shaved quills lay beside it.

"Forgive me, I have been writing letters all day."

Abe could not read ten words, but he casually picked up one of the reverend's pages and studied it.

"Who's this to?"

Higginson gently plucked it from the boy's fingers. "Another servant of God."

He sat down and asked Sarah for her story. She told him everything, from their flight from Maine to her father's work as a constable, and his growing dissatisfaction with the course of justice in Essex County.

"So your father refused to arrest more suspects," Reverend Higginson said. His hands lay folded together on the table, looking like they were carved from marble.

"He wasn't paid for all his work," Sarah added.

"A wise excuse, though not wise enough, it seems. Your father did not want to take more of his poor neighbors to prison, and used his dispute about back pay to disguise his pangs of conscience." The old man sighed. "His ploy was not enough to keep him from the attention of the afflicted, alas."

In Andover, Higginson explained, a local magistrate signed numerous warrants for the arrest of suspected witches until so many came to him that he refused to authorize any more. It was not long before the magistrate was denounced as a witch. He fled the county.

Sarah quaked with anger. She had seen the afflicted girls' fits. They were terrifyingly convincing, but the events of the past day made her doubt everything.

She said, "Is it all imposture?"

The reverend held up a page of one of his letters close to his face so his weak eyes could read it.

"The Devil is very real, my child. He is the most subtle of beings, but if his design was to destroy this Christian colony, he could do no worse than deceive us with visions of witchcraft."

All this time Abe had been standing silently to one side. He spied a tray laden with biscuits and butter. Sidling over, he went to help himself. Sarah scolded him, but Reverend Higginson laughed and offered to heat milk for them both.

While he was out of the room, Sarah whispered, "Witches or devils there may be, but I will not let them hang my father!"

"What can we do?" Abe replied.

"I don't know. I have to think."

Reverend Higginson returned with a pot of hot milk. Sarah and Abe had milk with their biscuits, and the reverend had English tea with his.

He invited Sarah to stay. Higginson's family and manservant were away visiting relatives. Abe and Sarah could do small things to help the old man, and he would shelter them so they could be near their imprisoned parents.

That night, before bed, Reverend Higginson prayed with them. He recited Psalm 142: "'Attend unto my cry; for I am brought very low; deliver me from my persecutors, for they are stronger than me. Bring my soul out of prison, that I may praise thy name; the righteous shall compass me about, for thou shalt deal bountifully with me.'"

In the dark, on a pallet in the kindly old man's front room, Sarah thought about the words of the Psalm: "bring my soul out of prison." There was no crime, and no sin, in freeing the innocent. Her father was innocent. She would find a way to free him.

That night she dreamed she and her father were pursued by Abigail Williams, Betty Hubbard, and the rest, screaming for blood. When Sarah splashed out to the passing boat for rescue, she found it filled with black-robed judges carrying nooses. They kept trying to draw ropes around Sarah's and her father's neck. She awoke bathed in sweat, as wet as if she had been swimming.

False dawn touched the shutters. Sarah's empty belly growled. Thinking of breakfast reminded her of where her father was being held. He would be hungry, too. She threw back the blanket and padded in her stockinged feet to the front door. Before she could lift the latch, a deep voice said, "Are you going out, child?"

Reverend Higginson was at his writing table, quill in hand. He was so quiet that she had no idea he was in the room. Her stomach rumbled again.

"The privy is out back," he said. He wrote with deft strokes, making no sound. "Or are you hungry?"

"I am, sir, but I was thinking of how to get breakfast to my father in jail."

"The guards will let you in. I will compose a note for you." He rummaged through the scattered papers and found a useful scrap. "I have a pail you may use to carry food and drink to your father."

Sarah felt like crying. "You are good to me, sir, and I am a stranger!"

"As our Lord said, 'I was a stranger, and ye took me in.'" He smiled. "Our lives are ordered by God, child. Your coming, like young Absalom's, has given clarity to some ideas I have been thinking for some time."

Reverend Higginson put down his pen. He held up a document, several pages long. "Some ministers of the gospel, myself included, are going to take a stand against the killing of our neighbors. The court has gone too far. It is taking the Devil's word against Christians', and that cannot be just."

Hearing this filled Sarah with hope. If ministers came out against the witch hunt, then there was hope for all those in jail.

Sarah and Reverend Higginson prepared a meal for Ephraim. They put bread, cheese, ham, and cider in the old man's bucket and covered everything with a cloth. With Higginson's note in hand, Sarah walked the block to Salem jail.

It was a hot morning. The night-duty jailer was still there when Sarah arrived. He could not read Reverend Higginson's note, being unlettered, but he was impressed it came from the revered minister. The jailer gave her bucket a brief examination and let her go.

Ephraim was in a large cell with a score of others. He was awake, his back propped against the wall. Seeing Sarah, he looked alarmed and delighted.

"You should not come here," he said in a low voice. Many were still asleep. "There is typhus in the jail." Typhus, or jail-fever, was what killed Sarah Osburn and Roger Toothaker, among others.

"I had to bring you decent food and drink," she replied.

Ephraim ate gratefully. He asked where Sarah had gotten the food, and where she had spent the night. She told her father about Reverend Higginson's charity to her and Abe Toothaker.

"All good men are not asleep!" he said. "I shall remember his kindness when I get out."

His promise made Sarah uneasy. "Father, how will you get out?"

"After my trial finds me innocent."

"No one has been found guiltless so far!" she reminded him. Ephraim ate silently for a while. Sarah lowered her voice to the smallest whisper.

"Suppose you escaped?"

"Others have tried. They were all caught." Sarah asked who had tried. "Sarah Good and a woman named Mary Green. They were goodwives, not stout soldiers."

Ephraim drained the last drops of cider. The bucket was empty. He felt around the bottom.

"Plenty of room," he muttered. He put the mug back in and covered it with the cloth.

"I shall need tools," he whispered. "A knife, and a saw of some kind. Even a piece of a saw blade would do." The bars and partitions in the jail were wood. Ephraim was not chained, because the jailers refused to let him go outside. With his obvious strength and agility, they did not want to take any chance of him running.

"I'll get them," Sarah vowed. "How soon should I return?"

"Don't come again today, lamb. It will look suspicious, plus the odor of this place will make you sick. Come tomorrow morning, just like today."

With a brief kiss on the forehead, he sent her on her way. The day jailer had come to work by then. He curtly ordered Sarah to present her pail for inspection. Finding only an empty cup, he let her go.

On her way back to Reverend Higginson's house, Sarah weighed whether she should tell her benefactor about the plot to free her father. She decided not to. First, she had no wish to involve the good Reverend in a crime. Second, if he did not approve, he might prevent her, or third, he might want to help, and the fewer involved in a plot, the easier it would go.

She did decide to recruit Abe. When she told him her plans later that day, he made only one condition for his help.

"We have to get my mother out, too," he declared.

Sarah was taken aback. Mary Toothaker was jailed far away, in Cambridge, near Boston. They had no way of reaching her, much less freeing her.

"If you won't help get my mother out, I won't help you get your father free!" Abe said.

"Shh! Lower your voice Abe!" They were in Reverend Higginson's yard, fetching water from his well. "I'll help you with your mother, but we must get my father out first," Sarah insisted. The Court of Oyer and Terminer was hearing cases in Salem jail first, as they were closest. "We can collect tools and things for both of them, can't we?"

Abe lifted a full bucket with both hands. Grunting, he asked, "What do we need?"

"A knife, my father said, and a saw blade, to start with. I still have Goodman Dodge's mule, though a horse would be faster." Sarah struggled to lift a full bucket of water. "Food for a journey, too."

"Where will we go?"

Sarah wobbled a few steps, then set the pail down. Where would they go?

"Reverend Higginson writes to ministers in New York," she said. "He says they are not so easily fooled by stories of specters and witches there." Sarah had only a vague idea where New York was, but her father could see them through to any destination.

"I want a weapon," Abe said. "A pistol or a sword."

The idea of Abe armed was absurd, but she tactfully did not say so. Abe agreed to find a knife and saw for her. She would collect food for four people.

Abe found a saw blade in less than a day. He went to a cabinet maker's shop and begged for a piece of broken saw blade. A knife proved harder to get. Knives cost money, and neither of them had any.

"Take one of the reverend's," Abe suggested.

"I won't steal from him!" Sarah replied.

"'Tisn't stealing if you give it back," the boy reasoned. Feeling desperate, Sarah reluctantly agreed. One way or another she would return the knife to Reverend Higginson.

It being summer, food was in ready supply, though a drought gripped Massachusetts. Sarah put aside half of everything she was offered. So did Abe. Reverend Higginson noticed and asked her why.

She did not want to lie to him. Lying was a grave sin, a breaking of faith. On the other hand, Sarah wanted to protect the old gentleman if her plot failed.

"I mean to leave soon," she said carefully. "I am saving food for the trip." Abe parroted her explanation.

Reverend Higginson smiled. "You can do better than save a few random scraps." He went to his larder and brought back a sack of dried beans, a small side of bacon, and half a hoop of cheese. Sarah thanked him profusely.

"'Tis nothing. When do you leave?"

She considered. "In a day or so."

"Are you leaving then, too, Absalom?"

Abe stammered yes.

"Where will you go, children?"

Lying to the old man was hard. Sarah said something about returning to Dr. Griggs, while Abe claimed one of his elder sisters would take him in.

"Will you not stay for your father's trial?"

Choosing her words carefully, Sarah said, "I could not bear to see my father on trial for his life."

Understanding glimmered in the old man's eyes. "I shall pray for your father and the judges, so that God may grant them truth."

As August came to an end, there were new sensations. William Barker of Andover made an elaborate confession about

his involvement in a diabolical conspiracy to overthrow the Colony of Massachusetts and create a Devil-worshipping nation in its stead. Barker said there were 307 witches in the colony, including an armed militia of male witches. His remarks told against Ephraim Wright. What better recruit for the Devil's plans than a soldier who could train the armed witches? After Barker's confession, Ann Putnam Senior began seeing the spirit of Ephraim Wright drilling the Satanic militia on every moonlit night.

Sarah took a food pail to her father each morning. The night jailer grew used to her and barely glanced at the bucket. His successor, the day jailer, was a much harsher man. Sarah decided to bring the tools to Ephraim early, before the day jailer came on duty.

On September 1, Ephraim was given a date for his examination: September 5. He told Sarah, and they agreed to try the escape Sunday morning, the fourth.

Abe would bring the mule and wait in the alley alongside the jail. Once Ephraim sawed his way out, he would escape to the alley, take the mule, and rendezvous with the children outside of town. Together they would make for Cambridge, free Mary Toothaker, and flee any way possible south to New York.

chapter twelve

The New World

Sarah and Abe rose before dawn. They crept around Reverend Higginson's front room, gathering their supplies, tools, and bucket. Abe slipped out to get the mule. Sarah spread a napkin over the food in the pail and started for the door.

"Early today, child?"

Like a ghost, the elderly minister stood in the darkened doorway of his bedroom, clad in a long white nightshirt.

"Begging your pardon, sir. Did we wake you?"

"Old men keep strange hours. I have been up awhile."

Sarah heard the clop-clop of the mule in the street. "I must be off," she said. With feeling, she added, "Thank you, sir."

"You are leaving?"

She held up the pail with both hands. It was heavier than usual.

"My father's breakfast."

"You are early today."

Sarah glanced out the door. "Am I? I did not sleep well."

"These are testing times. I am happy to have helped you and young Absalom. Good-bye. I will pray for you."

Did he know they were not coming back? His farewell sounded as final as Sarah's did.

Heart hammering, Sarah went out into the gray light before dawn. Abe held Kate's halter. He put all their supplies in an old flour sack and draped it over the mule's neck. Sarah hurried across the yard. Without a word, she strode past Abe.

"C'mon, mule," he said quietly.

A dog barked a few streets away. They took the shortcut opposite the town common, which brought them practically to the front door of the jail.

The morning air was thick with haze blown in from the sea. Walking fast, Sarah felt sweat trickle down the closed collar of her dress. She glanced back and saw she had outpaced Abe and the mule by half a block. She waited for them at the corner.

"Are you ready?" she asked.

"Wish I had a pistol," Abe grumbled.

"I am grateful you don't." In answer to his hurt expression, she said, "No one is supposed to get hurt. That means you, too, Abe." He grinned.

"Take Kate down the alley, tie her there, and go on by yourself," Sarah said.

"Where shall we meet?"

"The Beverly Ferry."

They clasped hands. Looking positively piratical, Abe skulked across the empty street, leading Kate to the alley alongside the jail. Sarah said a prayer for her father, then marched straight to the gate of the fence surrounding the jail.

It was locked.

She could see a number of prisoners sleeping outside on the ground. It was too hot and too crowded in the jail, so some of the accused were allowed to spend the night outdoors. They were shackled, and the gate was locked to keep them in. How was Sarah supposed to get inside?

Help arrived in an unexpected way. The day jailer, the very man Sarah had hoped to avoid, arrived early. Eyeing the girl by the gate, he demanded to know her business.

"My name is Sarah Wright. I bring breakfast to my father, Ephraim Wright. I do it every day."

The lanky jailer shoved a hand into a greasy coat pocket and brought out a ring of keys.

"Dutiful daughter, eh?" He unfastened the big brass padlock and swung the gate open. "After you."

"Thank you." Sarah eased by him, clutching the pail close to her chest. As she did, a distinct metallic clink escaped the container.

"Here, what you got there?"

"Food," Sarah replied, struggling not to stammer with fear.

"Let me see."

She lifted the napkin. As the jailer peered in, she deliberately tilted the pail so that the stoneware flagon of cider clattered against the brass handle. Underneath the sausage, cheese, and cider was a thin disk of wood Abe had sawed off a fence post.

Under it was one of Reverend Higginson's paring knives and a length of saw blade.

"Good breakfast," said the jailer. "Where d'you get the sausage?"

"The Ship Tavern," Sarah said. Her hands were starting to tremble, as much from fear as from the weight of the bucket.

"I like Beadle's better." He dropped the napkin. Sarah closed her eyes briefly and thanked the Lord.

The night jailer was his usual amiable self. He hailed Sarah and his relief. The day man questioned his colleague about Sarah. Did he know her?

"Surely!" the night jailer said. "She's Ephraim's girl. You know Ephraim; he broke up the fight in the gallery the other day." Apparently, Sarah's father had helped quell a disturbance. The day man grunted.

"Well, all right. Take him his tuck, and be quick about it."

Sarah found her father asleep by the rear wall. At her touch he bolted upright, fists clenched. Seeing Sarah, he relaxed.

"Lamb! I'm sorry! One has to sleep with one eye open in a place like this."

She set the bucket down. "Here's breakfast, Father. I pray you find it *nourishing*." This was the secret word they had agreed on to indicate that the escape was on.

Their eyes met, and Sarah lowered her gaze to the bucket significantly. Ephraim betrayed nothing. Other prisoners were all around, and some might be listening.

"Thank you, lamb. I am sure it will do me good."

They chatted a bit more, trying to sound casual. A bell pealed far away. It was Sunday. Sarah started at the sound. Ephraim held her hand.

"Go now," he said. "I shall see you soon."

He took out the contents of the bucket, carefully covering the tools with the napkin. Ephraim replaced the false bottom and handed the pail to Sarah.

"Good-bye, Father."

"Farewell, lamb."

The day jailer noticed the cloth was not in the bucket when she left. Sarah explained her father wanted to keep it to wipe his hands and face.

Outside, Sarah looked back as the jailer propped the door open with a stone. The wide opening was a black rectangle, revealing nothing of the despair within. *The door to Hell must look like that*, she thought.

Sarah forced herself not to look in the alley to see if the mule was tied there. She had to trust Abe to do his part. Down the lane, she went right onto the main street. Already the people of Salem were heading to meeting. Sarah mixed into the stream of people headed for the meetinghouse. She passed the Ship Tavern, then broke away down the side street until she had completely circled the jail. The road to the Beverly Ferry followed the shore of the North River. She steadied herself against going too fast. No sense attracting unwanted attention.

Along the North River, boats were moored to pilings or dragged up on the shore. No work was allowed on Sunday.

Sarah thought if they missed the ferry, they could take a boat, leaving it for the owner on the other side of the river.

A flock of crows flashed overhead. They settled on the shore, watching Sarah with beady black eyes. She remembered when she and her father first came to Salem Village, how the crows had followed them. Was it a good omen or an ill one that the black birds followed her departure?

The Beverly Ferry was not in when Sarah reached the landing. For a brief moment she feared it would not be running on the Sabbath, but when some men appeared who also intended to cross, she decided they must know the schedule better than she.

The ferry emerged from the morning haze, ghosting along under a small sail. No sign yet of Abe or her father. Sarah paced back and forth across the end of the pier, gnawing her lip. What if they had been caught?

The ferry docked. Two wagons came off, along with half a dozen people on foot. The men from Salem Town got on. There was no one else to board but Sarah. The ferryman, an African slave, called to her. Nervously, she shook her head no. The ferry cast off. The slave manned a sweep, and the ferry pulled away from the Salem shore.

Abe came running pell-mell down the path. Sarah wondered if every constable in Essex County was at his heels. He skidded to a stop in a cloud of dust, panting.

"Your father is out!" he gasped. "A great fight broke out in the jail just after he left!"

Apparently, other prisoners had discovered the spot where Ephraim had sawed the wooden bars away. Instead of taking turns creeping out, they started fighting about who would go first. The day jailer heard the commotion and summoned the guards. The indoor inmates, who were not shackled, put up a fight when the guards came in. As a result a full-blown battle broke out in the close confines of the crowded jail.

"Mercy!" Sarah said. "Did they notice my father was missing?"

"Nah," Abe said. "It'll be half a day before they are able to sort things out!"

Sarah was doubtful. She watched the main road and the riverside lane for any sign of her father. Her heart leaped when she saw the rusty brown mule coming down the river road, led by a sturdy, hatless man. She ran to meet him.

Ephraim was remarkably calm. He had changed the coat he had worn in prison for the garment Sarah had scrounged for him and left with the mule. It was a military coat, canvas-colored, with red facings. With his hair pulled back in an army-style queue, Ephraim looked like a soldier on fatigue duty—certainly not like an escaped prisoner.

He threw his arms around Sarah and lifted her off her feet.

"We did it!" she said, crushed against him.

"Only the first step." Others had broken out, only to be captured again.

With Abe, they went down to the ferry dock. The children were surprised when he said they were leaving the mule behind.

"She belongs to Goodman Dodge," Ephraim said. "Even if he did loan her to us, we cannot take her any farther. It would be theft." And theft, like witchcraft, was a hanging offense.

Kate was tied to a tree along the shore road, where she could graze until someone found her. Time crawled. After what seemed like hours, the ferry came into sight again, driven by the breeze from the Beverly shore. It docked. No one got off.

Ephraim muttered to the children, "If need be, deny you know me."

"Father!" Sarah objected.

"Do as I say!"

He strolled onto the boat well ahead of Sarah and Abe. To their surprise there was a single passenger on board, a clergyman dressed in black. Sarah's breath caught in her throat. She recognized Reverend Hale of Beverly.

Ephraim sat on the gunwale across from Reverend Hale, who read from a small book.

"Good day to you, reverend sir," Ephraim said boldly. Sarah and Abe drifted past. They sat down as far from Ephraim as they could.

Mr. Hale looked up from his reading.

"And to you, goodman. Are you bound for Beverly?"

"I am. And you, sir? You do not debark in Salem Town?"

Hale closed his book. "Alas, I am to preach in the meetinghouse this afternoon, but once on board the ferry I found I had left my sermon notes at home. So I must return to fetch them."

Ephraim leaned back against the rail. The ferryman cast off, and began the slow journey across the river.

"On what text will you preach?" Ephraim asked. Sarah listened to him making polite conversation and gnawed her lip.

"No specific text, but rather a discourse on the afflictions currently besetting our people," he replied.

"The French and the Indians?"

"No, I refer to our unfortunate plague of witchcraft." Sarah held her breath. Hale said, "You are a soldier, I take it?"

"I am. I go to join the war against the Wabanaki."

"May God protect you, sir! The Indians, I am told, fight as vicious devils. No wonder, since they worship the Prince of Darkness!"

"They are no worse than ourselves," Ephraim replied calmly. "They are fighting for their homes and land. As for their religion, I know nothing of it."

Hale smiled. He was a pleasant-looking fellow, neatly dressed and well-groomed.

"This treatise I was reading has many useful stories in it about the Devil and his works. You have heard of the Reverend Cotton Mather?" Ephraim nodded. "He has made a close study of the invisible world."

He handed the small book to Sarah's father. Ephraim read the title page and a few past it.

"Do you think such things can be? Witches, I mean, and evil magic?"

Hale spread his hands. "Without doubt, sir!"

"I wonder. If men are capable of great evil out of their own minds, what need is there in God's world for devils and witches?"

Hale's good humor faded. "You jest, sir! You cannot doubt the truth of the invisible world. To do so would cast doubt on everything, up to and including Christ Our Lord!"

Ephraim handed back the book. "I am a Christian, never fear."

"I rejoice! So many people these days lack faith, especially worldly men like yourself."

Ephraim let the conversation die. Abe went to the bow and waved his arms at the gulls hovering in front of the boat. Sarah watched the ferryman bent over his sweep to keep her eyes off her father. Ephraim slumped against the rail, head down as if dozing.

The north shore loomed ahead. Mr. Hale rose, dusted himself off, and moved to the shore end to disembark. Passing Sarah, he glanced her way, then looked again.

"Hello," he said. "You are a village girl, are you not?"

"Yes, sir."

"You too, lad?" he said, spying Abe at the rail. "Why are two children from Salem Village on the ferry to Beverly?"

Sarah had no answer. Abe was ready to bolt. Sarah glanced past Mr. Hale to the landing, where a number of people stood waiting for the boat.

One of them was Sheriff Corwin!

She looked at her father, still apparently napping amidships. Sheriff Corwin could not fail to recognize Ephraim, whom he knew was supposed to be in jail in Salem Town!

"We are on our way to my uncle's in Beverly," Abe said, stammering.

Abe saw the sheriff, too. His thin face contorted with anger. Corwin was the man who arrested his father and mother. Corwin confiscated property of accused witches for the county. Abe pulled Sarah away from Reverend Hale and whispered, "The sheriff! He knows us!" He was trembling. "What shall we do?"

Sarah looked past him at Corwin waiting on the dock. "When the Indians came to our farm, father and I survived because we were apart."

The ferry crept toward shore. When the gangplank was lowered, Abe hissed, "We are going to get caught!"

Sarah thought desperately. They had come so far. How unlucky were they to cross right when the sheriff of Essex County happened to be waiting at the landing?

Something in Abe's face changed. His thin brows pushed together in a serious frown.

"You are not going to be caught, you hear? I won't let you." She stared at him, puzzled. "Whatever happens, don't you stop."

"What do you mean?"

"You get clear of this place, you and your papa. If I get away, I'll meet you in Cambridge by the jail."

So saying, he picked up a wooden bucket off the deck, dashed quickly down the plank, and dragged it through the

muddy water. Before anyone could say or do anything, Abe Toothaker flung the water, bucket and all, at Sheriff Corwin and the men with him.

They shouted oaths at the boy. He dashed past them, thumbed his nose, and took off up the hill. Sheriff Corwin and the four men with him followed, waving sticks and vowing revenge.

Stunned, Sarah watched Abe lure the sheriff away. She was still gaping when Mr. Hale slipped past.

"Even the least of my children may have a noble heart, eh? Farewell, Miss Wright. I pray all will be well for you," he said.

She was shaken anew. Reverend Hale recognized her? Did he fail to recognize Ephraim, or did he simply choose not to denounce him to the law?

Reverend Hale crossed the dock in quick strides. Her father took her by the arm.

"Come, lamb. Let us not waste the gift Absalom has given us."

They went ashore. Ten days later, they were in New York, and free.

 the end

The Real History Behind the Story

Though infamous, the Salem witch trials are also clouded with myth and misunderstanding. By far the largest witch trials in English America, the Salem affair was a minor incident compared to the terrible witch hysteria that afflicted continental Europe in the sixteenth and seventeenth centuries. In parts of Germany, thousands of people were tortured and executed during the worst periods of persecution.

The Massachusetts Bay Colony

In 1692, Massachusetts was under great stress. The colonists had thrown out a royal governor, Edmund Andros, in 1689 for trying to bring direct royal rule to the previously self-governing colony. This coincided with the overthrow of King James II, a Catholic, in favor of his Protestant daughter Mary, married to the Dutch Prince William of Orange. James II was forced out, William and Mary became joint rulers, and King James' governor Andros was ousted. Massachusetts had to apply to the new monarchs in Britain for a charter under which their local government could legally operate.

A new governor, Sir William Phips, was a rough and ready soldier with little understanding of law or theology. His first concern was the deadly raids by the French and the Wabanaki Indians in what is now Maine. Sir William allowed the judges in Salem to handle the witch craze until so many people were accused it seemed as though the entire situation was out of control.

Before the witch craze in Salem, thousands of accused witches were executed in Europe during the sixteenth and seventeenth centuries. One method of execution was burning an accused witch at the stake.

The Salem Witch Trials

Twenty people were executed in Massachusetts. Nineteen were hanged, and one man, Giles Cory, was pressed to death under a pile of stones because he refused to answer the formal charges. Six of the executed were men; fourteen were women. At least five people died in jail, including Sarah Good's infant child. Those who confessed to witchcraft, like Tituba or Abigail Hobbs, were spared to face a future capital trial. By that time the mania had passed, and all charges against the confessors were dropped. All the people executed refused to admit any guilt. Once the hangings began, confessions multiplied when people realized it was one sure way to postpone death.

It was common a hundred years ago to blame the Massachusetts clergy, particularly Cotton Mather, for the witch craze. Reading the actual records of the time reveals a much different story. Though they were firm believers in the existence of the Devil and his works, Mather and other clergymen

Sir William Phips arrived in the Massachusetts Bay Colony in 1692 to serve as governor of Salem.

were against the court sentencing accused witches to death on "spectral evidence"—that is, the testimony of invisible scenes witnessed by the afflicted. It was not until the end of the summer of 1692 that their advice was heeded. The last hangings occurred on September 22.

The Aftermath

Accused witches languished in jail until the next year. Gradually, public and private opinion changed, and instead of witchcraft, blame for the events of 1692 was placed on the Devil. The authorities came to believe the afflicted girls and later victims were possessed by demons, not bewitched by magic. In other words, lying demons took control of the girls and accused innocent people, to confuse the righteous colonists and deceive them into killing their neighbors.

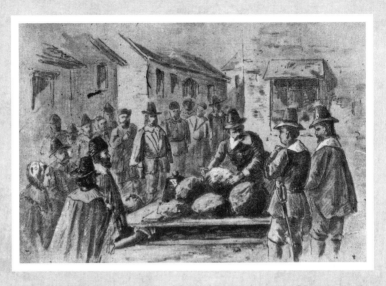

Giles Cory was pressed to death under a pile of heavy stones. Of the twenty people executed during the trials, Giles Cory was the only person executed this way because he refused to face the formal charges.

As adults, many of the girls (Ann Putnam Junior, for example) admitted publicly that they were wrong to accuse others of bewitching them. One exception to this seems to have been Abigail Williams. There is no record that she ever admitted any mistake. As late as the 1950s, the Massachusetts legislature has publicly apologized for the events of 1692.

More recently, attempts have been made to blame the hysteria on disease or environmental poisoning, such as eating contaminated bread. Such theories fail to match the known facts. The afflicted had fits, saw visions, and recovered until the next time. Poison and disease are not

After the hysteria ended in Salem, many people apologized for their role in the events. Judge Samuel Sewall had his apology read in front of his church congregation in 1697.

so accommodating. Fraud is another popular idea. While some fraud undoubtedly did occur, the behavior of the Salem Village afflicted was pathological. Responsible people in 1692 knew fraud when they saw it. The fits of the village girls were terrifying and properly should be seen as psychiatric cases.

Further Reading

Fiction

Duble, Kathleen Benner. *The Sacrifice*. New York: Margaret K. McElderry Books, 2005.

Fraustino, Lisa Rowe. *I Walk in Dread: The Diary of Deliverance Trembley, Witness to the Salem Witch Trials*. New York: Scholastic, 2004.

Hearn, Julie. *The Minister's Daughter*. New York: Atheneum Books for Young Readers, 2005.

Nonfiction

Aronson, Marc. *Witch-hunt: Mysteries of the Salem Witch Trials*. New York: Atheneum Books for Young Readers, 2003.

Fradin, Dennis Brindell and Judith Bloom Fradin. *The Salem Witch Trials*. Tarrytown, N.Y.: Marshall Cavendish Benchmark, 2009.

Nardo, Don. *The Salem Witch Trials*. Detroit, Mich.: Lucent Books, 2007.

Internet Addresses

Famous American Trials: Salem Witchcraft Trials 1692
<http://www.law.umkc.edu/faculty/projects/ftrials/salem/salem.htm>

National Geographic: Salem Witch Hunt—Interactive
<http://www.nationalgeographic.com/salem/index.html>

Salem Witch Trials Documentary Archive and Transcription Project
<http://www2.iath.virginia.edu/salem/home.html>